Buried Innocence

A MARY O'REILLY PARANORMAL MYSTERY

(Book Thirteen)

by

Terri Reid

"I didn't give you the gift of life,

But in my heart I know.

The love I feel is deep and real,

As if it had been so.

For us to have each other

Is like a dream come true!

No, I didn't give you

The gift of life,

Life gave me the gift of you."

Unknown

This book is dedicated to my daughters-in-law, Ann and Jori, who have allowed the blessings of adoption to touch our lives and hearts, and enrich our family. I love you!

BURIED INNOCENCE – A MARY O'REILLY
PARANORMAL MYSTERY
by
Terri Reid

Acknowledgements

The author would like to thank all those who have contributed to the creation of this book: Richard Reid, Sarah Powers, Virginia Onines, Denise Carpenter, Juliette Wilson, Maureen Marella, Donna Basch of the Galena-Jo Daviess County Historical Society & U.S. Grant Museum and Hillary Gadd.

She would also like to thank all of the wonderful readers who walk with her through Mary and Bradley's adventures and encourage her along the way. I hope we continue on this wonderful journey for a long time.

Prologue

Donna McIntyre's old car chugged up the hill, straining as it climbed the cobblestoned street leading to her apartment. She leaned forward in the driver's seat, willing the old, gas-guzzling Buick to keep moving. Glancing over to her son, Ryan, sitting in his car seat behind her, she smiled to herself as she saw he was leaning forward too. "We'll make it, right?" she asked him.

He nodded and with his six-year old wisdom added. "It's been a long day for Bertha. She's just tired, Mommy."

Donna had only spent $500 on Bertha Buick, and the car had been faithfully delivering them back and forth from their small apartment, to Ryan's daycare and then to Donna's workplace. She avoided adding any extra miles to Bertha's day, but they had run out of groceries and so had added an extra ten miles to drive back and forth to the grocery store. "I know, sweetheart," she agreed. "And she did a great job today. I promise once we park her for the night, she will be able to sleep for at least ten hours."

"Then she'll be happy," Ryan said with a satisfied nod.

Bertha coughed a few times but eventually made it up the hill and into the parking spot next to their apartment building. "Good job," Ryan said, patting the dashboard in front of him. "I'm very proud of you."

Donna grinned. Ryan had used the same words and inflection she used when she encouraged him. It was great to know that he actually heard what

1

she was saying. "Yes, Bertha did a great job," she agreed. "And now we need to carry our groceries upstairs and let her take a nap."

"I can help carry things," Ryan volunteered. "I have strong muscles."

"Excellent," she said. "Let's see if we can get everything in one trip."

She got of the car, reached into the backseat and unhooked Ryan from his car seat, and then opened the trunk of the car for the groceries. There weren't a lot of bags. Her tight budget only allowed for the necessities, but there were enough of the basics to keep them healthy and satisfy Ryan's growing appetite. She pulled out the lightest bag and gave it to Ryan. "Can you carry this one?" she asked.

He hefted the bag close to his chest and smiled up at his mom. "I've got it," he exclaimed with a wide smile. "See?"

She slipped her hands through the plastic openings in the bags and pulled the remaining eight bags from the back of the car. She tested and found them evenly balanced, then turned to Ryan. "You're doing a great job," she said to Ryan. "Now, can you hold on to my jacket, and we can walk together to the door, okay?"

Grabbing on to the hem of his mother's jacket, he nodded. "Okay," he said. "I'm ready."

They walked across the small parking lot to the front door. Donna was able to wedge open the door with her elbow and hold it open until Ryan was in. She looked up the steep staircase and sighed silently. Someday she was going to live on the first floor instead of the third one. Pasting a smile on her face, she turned to Ryan. "Ready for the climb up the mountain?" she asked.

Smiling and nodding, he moved to the staircase. "Maybe there will be snow on the top of the mountain," he said, stepping up in front of her.

"Or maybe a mountain lion," she replied, following him up.

"Or maybe a giant eagle," he suggested as he climbed slowly up the stairs.

"Or maybe a wizard," she added.

He nodded as he pulled himself up the stairs, using his free hand on the banister. "A wizard would be cool," he said. "And maybe he could use magic, and we could fly up the stairs."

"That would be cool," Donna agreed. "And maybe he could turn our apartment into a palace."

Ryan climbed a few more stairs, thinking about her comment before he responded. "But, Mom, if our apartment is turned into a palace, would Liza still be there?"

She smiled. Liza was Ryan's imaginary friend, and he had been weaving amazing tales about conversations he had with her. She was pleased to see that he had such a great imagination. "Well, I'm sure Liza could come with us," she agreed. "After all, she's part of our family."

"Yeah, Liza doesn't have her own family anymore," he replied thoughtfully.

They finally made it to their floor, and they walked over to the door. She unlocked it, pushed open the door and flipped on the light. "Why don't you play for a few minutes while I put the groceries away and start dinner," she suggested.

Ryan dropped the bag he was holding just inside the door and ran into the small living room. "I'm going to play school with Liza, okay?" he asked.

Bending to scoop up one more bag, Donna took a deep breath, willing the tiredness to go away and nodded. "That sounds great, sweetheart," she said.

Placing the bags on the counter, she slipped off her jacket and hung it on the back of a kitchen chair. Then she pulled an apron over her work clothes and started unpacking the groceries, first putting the refrigerated foods away and then working on the canned goods. She smiled as she heard Ryan singing. It wasn't a tune she was familiar with, so he must have learned it in daycare.

"Where did you learn that song?" she asked him, leaning over the open counter to listen more closely to the words.

"Liza taught it to me," he said.

She smiled. "Well, say thank you to Liza for me," she replied. "It's a pretty song."

He continued singing, "*Who will wipe away my tears? Who will chase away my fears? Who will sing me to sleep at night? Who will tuck me in real tight? Now that Momma's dead and gone, now that Momma's dead and gone.*"

Slightly alarmed at the lyrics, Donna walked around the counter and entered the living room. "How would you like to watch your favorite cartoon?" she asked, picking up a DVD on a shelf next to the television set and sliding it into the DVD player.

"But Liza still wants to sing," Ryan said.

"Well, Liza can sing, and you can watch television," she said. "How's that for a compromise."

He nodded. "I guess that will be fine."

She turned on the television and waited until Ryan's show started before returning to the kitchen to put away the rest of the groceries. She opened up a

4

cupboard and was reaching up to the top shelf to put an extra jar of peanut butter away when she heard the soft voice behind her. It was high-pitched, like a little girl's voice, but it held an ethereal quality to it as it filled the kitchen.

"Who will wipe away my tears? Who will chase away my fears? Who will sing me to sleep at night? Who will tuck me in real tight? Now that Momma's dead and gone, now that Momma's dead and gone."

Donna's heart was pounding, and her hands clutched the countertop. She was breathing heavily and was too frightened to move. Suddenly she felt a cold wash of air on her neck, and she held her breath.

"Momma's dead and gone," the ghostly voice whispered in her ear. "Dead and gone."

Chapter One

Mary O'Reilly was just finishing up a long day of paperwork at the office. Her desk was filled with an odd assortment of items: an opened and half-eaten sleeve of saltine crackers, a jar of peanut butter with a knife sticking out of the top, some slices of cheese, a jar of olives, some pieces of dark chocolate, a laptop with a spreadsheet program open, a large pile of assorted receipts, several files stuffed with paperwork, a bank statement, and a lit scented candle that smelled like evergreens.

But instead of working on accounting, she was absorbed with the computer screen in front of her. Mike appeared on the other side of her desk and sat in the chair.

"What's so interesting?" he asked casually.

Mary jumped and then looked around her monitor to the guardian angel. "I really wish you would knock or something," she said.

"You would think having ghosts appear to you at all times of the day or night would have cured you of being jumpy," he replied. "So, what are you looking at?"

"My horoscope," she said, lowering her voice in embarrassment and hiding back behind her monitor.

"Your horoscope?" he asked. "You don't believe in that stuff, do you?"

She peeked out again. "Well, most people don't believe in ghosts, and you can see how wrong they are," she argued. "Besides, I don't really believe in them. I just check them every so often. Just in case."

"Just in case of what?"

"Just in case they are true," she admitted sheepishly.

Laughing, he leaned back in the chair. "So, what's up in your horoscope?" he asked.

She shook her head and glanced at the screen again. "It's not good," she said, and then she read from the screen. "Caution is the key word for this week. The alignment of the planets for your sign set up a situation where bad luck could be the dominating force. Avoid tempting the fates. A black cat could be in your future."

"Wow, you're right," Mike replied. "You sit there, and I'll call Bradley to come and get you. We'll wrap you in bubble-wrap, and you can stay in your bedroom all week. Okay?"

"No one likes a smart-aleck," she said, wrinkling up her nose at him. "Fine, I'll just go back to work and not worry about my impending doom."

Popping an olive into her mouth, she picked up the receipt on the top of the file and looked it over. "Okay, May 15th, fifteen pounds of garlic," she said slowly. "Why did I buy fifteen pounds of garlic? And why did I consider it a business expense?"

"That was for the group that thought their ghost was also a vampire," Mike replied, the hint of a smile in his voice. "The only way they were going to let you investigate is if you wore a necklace of garlic, and, once they found out you were pregnant, you also wore a belt of garlic around your waist."

Mary nodded at him in a perfunctory manner. "Of course, that makes perfect sense," she said, adding the amount to the correct column in the spreadsheet. "Thank you, Michael."

"You are welcome, Mrs. Alden," he chuckled as he shook his head. He then took the time to examine the snacks she had scattered over her desk. "Looking at the assortment on your desk, if I had a stomach, I know I'd be sick to it."

Mary looked up at him and grinned. "I know. My tastes have certainly become eclectic," she admitted. "And you don't even want to look in the refrigerator."

"I thought the whole thing with pregnancy and weird cravings was an urban myth," he said.

Mary pulled another olive out of the jar and then absently smeared peanut butter on it before popping it into her mouth. "Yeah, me too," she said, picking up another receipt and studying it.

Mike shuddered. "Do you know what you just ate?" he asked with disgust.

Turning to him, confusion on her face, she shook her head. "What?"

"Never mind," he replied, moving his chair farther away from her. "So, are you going home soon?"

"Well, Bradley and Clarissa have an appointment with Dr. Springler this afternoon, and then they are going to go out for dinner together," she said. "Kind of a daddy-daughter date. So, this is the perfect time for me to go through my paperwork before I forget why I bought this stuff."

Mike leaned forward in the chair and studied her. "How are you feeling about things at home?" he asked.

She put the receipt down and turned her full attention to Mike. "Actually, I feel great," she admitted. "The food I'm eating is actually staying down. I've moved past my first trimester, so things are less scary for me. Clarissa seems to be responding really well to therapy. Bradley…well, Bradley is a little overprotective. But I get that, so I'm putting up with it."

She grinned. "And then I've got this great guardian angel who checks in on me…" she glanced over to the clock on the wall, "about every two and a half hours. It's endearing but getting slightly annoying."

Mike smiled sheepishly. "I was trying to cut back to every three hours," he admitted. "But I just get worried. This is my first pregnancy."

Shaking her head, she sat back in her chair. "I promise that I won't let anything important happen without calling you first," she said. "But in the meantime, I really need to get some work done. And with all these interruptions—"

The tone of her cell phone interrupted her, and sighing dramatically, she reached over to answer it.

"Mary O'Reilly."

She paused for a moment, and a smile spread across her face. "Amelia, it's good to hear from you," she said. "How's the ghost tour business going?"

Amelia was the owner of the popular and thriving Amelia's Ghost Tours in Galena, Illinois, a town about 45 minutes to the west of Freeport. Mary had met Amelia when she was in Galena looking for unique furnishings for her home when she first moved to Freeport. She caught sight of the store name and just had to go in. They became friends immediately.

"Business is great," Amelia replied. "But I've got something a little more paranormal than I'm equipped to handle. I know it's late, but do you think you could drive to Galena tonight?"

Mary glanced up at the clock. It was nearly five-thirty, but she could be there in an hour. "Sure, I can be there by six-thirty," she said. "Do you want to fill me in before I get there?"

Amelia paused for a moment. "No," she finally replied. "I think I'll let the woman sitting in my store tell you her own story. Then you can get her vibe on your own."

"So, do you think she's a nutcase?" Mary asked.

"Are you kidding me?" Amelia replied, and Mary could hear the laughter in her voice. "I run ghost tours for a living, and I'm calling a woman who talks to ghosts. Who the hell am I to judge?"

Mary laughed. "Excellent point," she said. "I'll see you in an hour."

Mary hung up the phone and looked up to see Mike's disapproving face glowering down on her. "Where do you think you're going, young lady?" he asked.

Mary stood, picked up her phone and purse and moved around her desk. "Um, to Galena," she replied, "to do my job."

"You think you can just drive off to Galena, in your condition?"

"Mike, I'm four months pregnant," she said. "For the most part, I feel great. I'm driving forty-five minutes away, on a lovely summer day with no rain in the forecast for days."

She walked out the door onto the sidewalk, and the hot August heat enveloped her. She was so glad her car had good air conditioning. When she turned and locked her office, Mike glided through the wall to stand next to her.

"Things could happen," he warned. "All kinds of things could happen."

She shook her head again. "Oh, so now you believe in my horoscope?" she asked, walking over to her parked car.

"No, I don't," he argued. "But there are other things out there that could harm you."

She paused on the sidewalk and looked at him. "Like what?"

He thought about her question for a moment. "Well, this could be a trap," he invented. "Amelia could have been forced to call you."

"I don't think many people could force Amelia to do something she didn't want to do," Mary said. "Besides, we have a code phrase just in case something like that happens."

Impressed, Mike glided up next to her. "You do?" he asked.

She nodded. "Yeah, it's 'Mike's paranoid,'" she replied. "Great phrase isn't it? Rings true."

He slipped in front of her to bar her way into the car. "Mary, you're not going," he said. "Final word on the subject."

She stopped and then moved to walk around him when she found her way blocked by scaffolding left there by window-washers. Dare she walk under a ladder when her horoscope just warned her to beware?

"Yeah, go ahead and walk under a ladder," Mike taunted.

Turning back, she reached through him, opened the door and slipped inside.

"Hey!" he cried. "Watch your hands."

"Sorry, a woman's got to do what a woman's got to do," she said, putting the key in the ignition and turning the car on.

Sliding through the passenger door to sit beside her, Mike folded his arms and sent her a determined look. "Well, you're not going without me," he stated.

Mary shrugged. "Fine," she replied, shifting into reverse.

A knock on the driver's side window startled her, and she turned to see a young woman standing in the street next to her car. She had long, dark hair and was dressed in mostly black. Mary rolled down the window and smiled. "Can I help you?" she asked.

The woman studied her for a moment, a cautious smile on her face, and then slowly nodded. "I just wanted to be sure you were okay before you drove off," the woman replied.

"Okay?" Mary asked.

"Well, yes," the woman answered. "I've been watching you from my store across the street, and it looked as if you were arguing with yourself about something."

Emitting a nervous laugh, the woman paused for a moment. "Well, I just wondered if you were having, you know, a nervous breakdown or something. I wanted to be sure you were okay before you got behind the wheel of your car."

Chuckling next to her, Mike sat back in the chair. "Sorry about that, Mary."

Taking a deep breath, Mary nodded to the woman. "How embarrassing," she said. "I realize that I must have looked a little odd from across the street. Every time I use my Bluetooth earpiece people think I'm talking to myself. Either I'm going to have to get a shorter hairstyle or a bigger ear piece."

The woman sighed with relief. "Of, of course, how silly of me," she apologized. "I am so sorry for delaying you."

"Oh, no problem. It was lovely to meet you," Mary said. "I'm Mary O'Reilly, and I am a private investigator."

"I'm Aubrie Ann," she said. "I run the New Age shop across the street. We just opened a couple of weeks ago."

"I'll have to come in and shop," Mary said. "That sounds interesting."

The woman stepped back and smiled down at Mary. "You have a very interesting aura," she said. "I'd love to have you stop by."

With a quick wave, Mary pulled out into the street and drove away.

"An interesting aura," Mike replied. "See, that's the kind of line I needed to know about when I was alive."

Mary glanced at him before she turned right on Business 20 to head out of town. "You used lines?" she asked.

He nodded. "Yeah, I had a few oldies but goodies that seem to charm the ladies."

"I know I'm going to regret this," she said. "But which one worked the best for you?"

He thought about it for a moment. "Well, it's been a while, but I think this one worked the very best," he said, and then he turned to her and winked. "Hey baby, if I told you I thought you had a gorgeous body, would you hold it against me?"

"No, that one couldn't have worked," she laughed. "Try again."

"I seem to have lost my phone number. Would you mind lending me yours?" Mike attempted.

"Nope, try again."

"If being sexy was a crime, you'd be guilty as charged!"

13

"Lame, really lame."

"Okay, I suddenly remembered my number one, works all the time, pick-up line," Mike said, a wide grin on his face.

"I know I'm going to be sorry," Mary said, easing into the right lane before turning onto Highway 26. "But go ahead."

Mike waited until Mary had lifted her bottled water to her lips and taken a sip. "Baby," he said, lowering his voice into a sexy purr and leaning towards her. "If you were a booger, I'd pick you first."

Water spewed from her mouth onto the steering wheel. "That was so not fair," she laughed as she coughed and wiped her eyes with her sleeve. "But now I totally understand."

"Understand what?" he asked.

"Why you thought the aura line was so great," she said. "And you're right. You really needed it."

"Harsh, Mary," he replied with a chuckle. "Really harsh."

Chapter Two

Amelia's Ghost Tours was located on Main Street in downtown Galena, and as Mary turned right from Highway 20 onto historic Main Street she immediately started scanning the street for parking. The small town was a tourist mecca with cobblestoned streets, quaint shops and historic buildings, so parking was often at a minimum especially when the crowds from Chicago traveled up for a long weekend. But, since this was a Monday evening, she was able to find a spot not too far from the picturesque shop in the middle of the block.

Walking uphill towards the shop, she inhaled deeply, enjoying the scents that where uniquely Galena. The Galena River was only a block away, and the hot summer wind carried its scent through the downtown street, enhanced by the smells emanating from the various shops on the street: popcorn, chocolate, steaks and pizza. It was a pregnant woman's olfactory bouquet.

"Remind me to get some popcorn before I leave," she whispered to Mike.

"Yeah, like I really will have to remind you," he teased.

She grinned. "Okay, remind me that the car is parked two blocks from the Popcorn Shop," she said. "And that I have to carry whatever I buy."

He smiled at her. "That I can do."

They stopped outside of Amelia's, and Mary turned to Mike. "Would you mind waiting for me outside?" she asked. "Amelia tends to get choked up when there are paranormal entities nearby."

"You mean she gets emotional?" Mike asked.

Mary shook her head. "No, ghosts make her cough," she explained. "I'm not sure how she'd react to a guardian angel, but just in case…"

"No problem," he said. "I'll just keep an eye on you through the window."

Entering the narrow store, Mary immediately saw the woman and her young son sitting on a small couch in the alcove, talking to Amelia who sat across from them on a small chair. When the bell over the door rang, Amelia looked up and smiled. "Mary, you made great time," she said. "How was the drive?"

"Gorgeous, as usual," she replied, and then she turned to the woman. "Hi. I'm Mary O'Reilly."

The woman took a deep breath before responding but pasted a shaky smile on her face. "I'm Donna, Donna McIntyre, and this is my son, Ryan."

"Hi Ryan," Mary said, smiling at the little boy. "What can I do for you?"

"Have a seat, Mary," Amelia insisted, pulling another chair close to the couch. "Donna had an interesting experience this evening that has her slightly freaked out, and I can't blame her."

Mary sat down and faced Donna. "So, what happened?"

After listening to Donna's recounting about hearing the voice, Mary turned to Ryan. "Was that your friend Liza singing?" she asked.

Ryan nodded casually. "Yeah, she likes to sing," he said. "I think that's a girl thing."

Mary smiled. "Yes, I agree," she said. "Have you talked to Liza about why she visits you so much?"

"She can't find her other mom, so she's just staying with us," he replied.

16

"What do you mean, other mom?" Mary asked.

"She was an orphan," he said. "And she got sent to one mom. Then she got sent to another place 'cause her new mom got sick. Then that place sent her to another place, and that's where she died."

"How did she die?" Mary asked.

"She doesn't like to talk about it," Ryan replied. "It makes her scared."

"Did she ever live in your apartment?" Mary asked. "Before you lived there?"

The little boy shook his head. "No, she was just taking a walk and saw us," he said. "She asked me if she could come home with us, and I told her yes. I knew Mom wouldn't mind. She's always helping people."

Mary smiled and glanced at Donna who was staring at her son in astonishment. "Ryan, why didn't you tell me?" she asked.

"I did," he said. "Remember? I said I had a new friend and she wanted to come home with us. And you said okay."

Donna closed her eyes and inhaled softly. "You're right, I did," she finally said. "I remember now, we were visiting your grandparents. But I thought your friend was imaginary."

Ryan shook his head. "Nope, she was just invisible," he said matter-of-factly.

"Oh, that's all," Amelia inserted and then turned to Mary. "So, can you help them?"

Mary turned back to Ryan. "Has Liza ever told you to do anything bad or dangerous?" she asked.

"No, she's pretty quiet and likes to hide," he said. "I was real surprised when she sang to Mom. She must like her."

17

"She must trust her," Mary added, turning to Donna. "Whoever is staying with you doesn't seem to be threatening or malicious. She just seems to be lost or looking for someone."

"Well, that's a relief," Donna said. "She really scared me."

"That's totally understandable," Mary agreed. "It sounds like she needs some more information until she can move on. Would you mind if I spoke with her?"

Donna shook her head. "No, please, I would feel better to have someone else hear what I heard," she agreed. "And Amelia told me about what you do. So, I think it would really ease my mind."

"Would you like me to come now?" Mary asked.

Nodding eagerly, Donna breathed a sigh of relief. "That would be wonderful," she replied. "I wasn't sure how I was going to face going back into my apartment."

"Great," Mary said. "Let's go."

Chapter Three

"So, where are we going?" Mike asked as Mary stepped out of Amelia's store.

Mary glanced over her shoulder to see that Donna and Ryan were still talking to Amelia and then whispered to Mike. "They have a ghost in their apartment, a little girl who is looking for her adoptive mother," she explained. "The ghost has been communicating with the little boy, but tonight she whispered to the mother."

"That probably freaked her out," Mike said.

"Exactly," Mary replied.

"Exactly what?" Donna asked as she stepped up beside Mary on the sidewalk.

Sighing, Mary glanced over to Mike who shrugged his shoulders and then back to Donna. "I was just telling my associate about your encounter this evening. He said that it probably freaked you out, and I said 'exactly,'" she replied.

"Oh, you have one of those Bluetooth things, don't you?" Donna asked.

"Why, yes I do," Mary said brightly. "Don't they come in handy at the most opportune times?"

"Yes, except people often think you're talking to yourself," Donna replied.

"Or your invisible friends," Mary added with a secret wink at Mike. "So, are we walking to your place?"

"Yes, it's just down at the end of Main Street," she replied. "Do you mind walking?"

Mary shook her head. "No, it's a lovely evening for a walk."

They walked together, Ryan chatting non-stop about the stores and his favorite places to window shop. As they crossed Hill Street, while looking out for traffic, Mary caught a movement out of the corner of her eye. She stopped and looked up the narrow, steep street again but didn't see anything. Maybe she'd take a little more time to check things out when she walked back to her car.

They arrived at the apartment, and Donna sighed. "Now we have three floors to climb," she murmured apologetically. "I'm so sorry."

Mary shook her head. "Don't worry about it," she said. "After the walk and the climb, I can justify a stop in one of the chocolate shops on my way back to my car."

The walk up the steps was easier without the grocery bags Donna and Ryan had carried earlier, but it was still no walk in the park. By the time they reached the door, they were all slightly out of breath. "I can see you don't need a gym membership," Mary said, panting softly. "This is quite a workout."

Donna smiled. "Well, that's one advantage to living up here."

She unlocked the door, and they all stepped inside. Mary slowly looked around the apartment. It was neat and tidy, but she could tell that most of the furniture was either second-hand or purchased from the local big-box store. Then she saw the little girl kneeling by the play table in front of the television. She looked to be about five years old. She had long, blonde hair, a petite bone structure and was wearing a nightgown that reached her knees. Mary thought she was a pretty little girl, but when she turned and looked up, Mary's stomach clenched. Taking a deep breath, Mary recalled the years of police training and pushed herself to stay mentally detached.

The subject has blue eyes, Mary noted silently, with two periorbital hematomas or, in layman's terms, black eyes. She has further ecchymosis or bruising on the face, neck and arms. There is also a sign of blunt force trauma to the side of her head, which could be the cause of death.

She didn't die fast enough from the choking, so she was battered against the wall. Mary felt the bile rising in her throat when Mike stepped up next to her. "Breathe Mary," he said. "Breathe deeply."

She turned away from the little girl and took a slow deep breath.

"Can you see her?" Donna asked.

Mary nodded wanly. "Yes. Yes, I can," she whispered.

"She looks pretty bad, don't she?" Ryan asked.

Mary nodded again. "Yes, she does," she replied, squatting down to face the little boy. "Did she ever frighten you?"

He shrugged easily. "Naw, my dad made my mom look kinda like that sometimes," he said with the openness and honesty that only a child can have, "until we ran away from him."

"Ryan, please," Donna said, mortified. "He didn't mean that. Please…"

Mary stood and turned to Donna. "Are you safe now?" she asked simply.

The air went out of Donna and she nodded slowly. "Yes, thank you," she said softly. "We're safe. It's been a long time since… I didn't know he still remembered."

"The little girl, his friend," Mary explained. "She was abused, badly. But Ryan still accepted her as a friend. That's why she trusted you."

A tear slid down Donna's cheek, and she quickly brushed it away. "Well, I suppose some good can come from all kinds of bad situations."

Nodding, Mary placed her hand on Donna's arm. "Yes, it can," she said, and then she looked over her shoulder. "I need to talk to her if that's alright with you?"

"Yes…please," Donna urged. "Find out what happened."

Mary moved across the room and sat down on the floor next to the toy table. "Hi. I'm Mary. I'm Ryan's friend," she said. "Can I be your friend, too?"

The little girl shyly looked at Mary with downcast eyes through the curtain of her hair and nodded.

"That's great," Mary said softly. "Ryan told me you were looking for someone, and I want to help."

Still holding her head down, the girl nodded again.

"Can you tell me who you want me to find for you?" Mary asked.

"My new mommy," the little girl said, her voice a mere whisper. "The new mommy that loved me."

She lifted her head slightly and met Mary's eyes with her large, sad ones. Her lips were trembling, and a large tear splashed from her eye onto her bruised cheek. "She gave me away," she continued softly. "She gave me away to the man who hurt me."

Then the little girl faded away.

Chapter Four

They waited for another twenty minutes, but Liza did not come back.

"She does that sometimes," Ryan said. "She gets sad and goes away for a while."

Mary had explained to Donna what the little girl had said, and now, instead of fearing the ghost, Donna was eager to help solve her mystery. "What should we do?" she asked Mary.

"Well, it would be very helpful if she could give us any more information," Mary said. "If she comes again, ask for her last name, her birthday, the town she used to live in or any other information that would help us identify her and her family."

Donna turned to her son. "Next time Liza comes, can you help me ask her some questions?"

Ryan nodded. "Sure, I can do that," he said, and then he turned to Mary. "Then Liza won't be sad anymore?"

"I'm going to try to make her happy again," Mary said. "I promise."

"Okay, then I'll ask her," he promised.

A few minutes later, Mary and Mike were standing on the sidewalk in front of their apartment building. The sun was setting, and the sky was the lavender color it gets just before it slides into the indigo of night. The street was quieter, more deserted, and Mary and Mike began their walk towards her car. "That was rough," Mike said, moving in step with Mary. "How are you doing?"

"I really thought I was going to lose it when I saw what some monster did to that poor little girl," she admitted, glancing up to him. "Thank you for coming to the rescue."

He smiled at her. "No problem," he said. "What's a guardian angel for if he can't come to the rescue every now and then. So, what's our next step?"

"Well, I really don't have a whole lot to go on yet," she said. "All I know is that we have a little girl, probably five or six, whose name is Liza. Her clothing appears to be somewhat modern, so I think she was probably murdered sometime in the past five years. And, because of the way she referred to a "new mom" she was either adopted or in the foster system."

"For the few minutes you had with her, I think you did a great job," Mike said. "And you not only connected with her, you helped that family."

"Well, I hope I did," she said. "And I hope Liza comes back so we can learn more about her and help her move on."

She started to cross Hill Street when she paused and looked up the narrow lane towards the top of the hill.

"What?" Mike asked.

"I thought I saw something up this way earlier," she replied. "I just want to be sure."

They walked up the steep incline of Hill Street and stopped when they reached Bench Street, halfway up the hill.

"Do you see anything?" Mike asked.

Mary, still straining her eyes in the dusky light, shook her head. "No, I don't," she replied. "And what I saw earlier was kind of weird anyway."

"In what way?"

"It was like I saw a half a person coming out of the hill," she said. "All I could see was his body from the waist up, and then he was gone."

"Okay, that was weird," Mike agreed. "I bet it was the peanut butter and olives. That would make anyone see weird things."

Laughing, Mary shook her head and then stopped suddenly. "That reminds me," she exclaimed.

"What?" Mike asked, slightly concerned.

"I'm starving! Let's get back to Main Street so I can get something good to eat."

She started to turn back, but out of the corner of her eye she caught sight of someone standing in the middle of Bench Street farther down the road. "There he is," she called, hurrying down the street. "That's the man I saw."

He was nearly a block down the street, so Mary could only make out his height and general build. But as she got closer, her steps slowed, and her stomach turned once again that night. "I know him," she whispered. "He appeared on the end of my bed a couple of months ago."

"Gross. What do you think happened to him?" Mike asked.

The skin on his face had been mostly peeled away, exposing bone and muscle. His clothing was eaten away too, leaving exposed patches of reddened skin in some places but deeper wounds and openings in other places.

Mary continued to move towards him. "Can I help you?"

He seemed surprised that she could see him. "You can see me?" he asked.

She nodded. "Yes, I can," she replied. "And I want to help you."

25

Suddenly she was nearly overcome by a powerful smell of sewage. She clapped her hand over her mouth and nose, trying not to gag. The man watched her and shook his head sadly. "Please, tell them to find me," he pleaded as he began to fade away. "I don't want to be buried here."

Chapter Five

"Hey sweetheart, how was your trip to Galena?" Bradley asked as Mary walked into the house.

"Well, it was very…interesting, to say the least," she replied, placing her purse and briefcase on the hall table before she walked over and slipped her arms around him. He wrapped his arms around her and held her for a moment, placing a kiss on the top of her head.

"Not interesting in a good way," he murmured as he continued to hold her.

Sighing softly, she snuggled closer, comforted by his scent and the strong beat of his heart. "I am always amazed at how depraved this world can be," she said. "It's a scary place out there."

He placed his cheek on the top of her head and was silent for a moment. Finally, he spoke. "There are bad things out there, and in our jobs we tend to see more than most people," he agreed. "But I think it's important that we remember that the good guys still outnumber the bad ones."

She nodded against his chest. "She was five or six," she whispered. "Only a few years younger than Clarissa. Whoever killed her beat her first, then strangled her, and then finally crushed her skull."

She could feel Bradley's arms unconsciously tightening around her. "How can I help?" he asked, his voice tight with anger.

She slipped her arms up around his neck and tiptoed so she could cover his mouth with her own.

He pulled her closer and returned her kiss, offering comfort and passion simultaneously.

"You already have helped," she whispered against his lips. "Just understanding, being angry too. It helps."

He hugged her tightly and then released her. "Now, to more practical matters," he said, his voice tender with love. "Have you eaten anything lately?"

She shook her head. "I was going to eat, but we had another encounter that sort of turned my stomach," she said. "But really, I'm starving now."

"Great," he replied, pleased by her response, "because Clarissa and I went to This Is It Eatery, and we brought you home take-out."

He hurried back into the kitchen and pulled a white styrofoam carton from the countertop and carried it back. Then he unlatched the lid from the bottom and let it flip open of its own accord. "Look! Ribs!" he declared. "Your favorite."

Mary looked at the meat hanging off the bones lying in the bottom of the container, the mottled red barbecue sauce slathered across the ribs, and instantly the image of the ghost in Galena came to mind. She clapped her hand over her mouth and dashed to the bathroom.

Bradley stared after Mary in confusion. "What? I thought you liked ribs!" he called after her.

Mike appeared behind Bradley, peeked over his shoulder and saw the offered dinner. "Not a good choice today," he said, shaking his head in sympathy. "Just not a good choice."

A few minutes later, Mary, a little worse for wear, stumbled out of the bathroom with a wan smile on her face. "Sorry. Just a bad day for ribs," she managed.

Bradley came forward, put his arm around her shoulders and led her to the kitchen table. "Yeah, Mike told me," he said. "Sorry about that."

She sat down and shrugged. "How were you supposed to know I'd had a personal encounter with a ghostly half-rack?" she asked. "Just bad timing. That's all."

He placed a hot cup of tea in front of her and handed her a chocolate protein bar. "Here," he said. "Eat this. It will get protein into your body, and you don't have to smell it."

Unwrapping the bar, she took a bite and smiled at him. "Thanks. This is just what I needed," she said, feeling the queasiness subsiding.

He sat down next to her, watching her as she finished the bar and then spoke. "So, do you want to talk about the other ghost?" he asked.

"No, not yet," she said, shaking her head. "I'd really like to check on Clarissa and then soak in the tub for a little while."

Leaning over her, he pressed a kiss on her forehead and nodded. "But remember, you can't have the water—"

"Too hot," she inserted, looking up at him and shaking her head. "Yes, Papa Bradley, I'll be sure to follow doctor's orders."

He grinned, slightly embarrassed. "Okay, maybe I'm a little overprotective," he said.

She stood up and pressed her lips to his. "You are just perfect," she said. "I don't mind a little pampering."

Holding her close, he just held her for a moment. "I'll remember that when you start complaining," he whispered.

"Well, okay," she admitted with a half giggle, half sigh. "I'll change it to 'I don't mind a little pampering on my terms.'"

Chuckling, he kissed the top of her head and stepped away. "Too late," he said. "The words have already been spoken."

He picked up her cup of tea and handed it to her. "Now go on up and visit with Clarissa," he said. "I know she's waiting up for you. I'll bring you a refill for your tea in a few minutes."

"Thanks," she replied. "I'll see you upstairs."

Chapter Six

Mary could hear voices when she got to the top of the stairs. She walked softly to the door of Clarissa's bedroom, paused, and listened, not wanting to interrupt anything important.

"But you still haven't answered my question," Clarissa said, exasperation evident in her young voice. "Where do babies come from?"

"Well, I really think that's a question for your mom or dad," Mike nervously replied. "It's not something you should discuss with your guardian angel, especially me."

"You know, don't you?" she asked.

Mike paused, and Mary stifled a laugh.

"Well, yeah, I know," he admitted.

"So, why won't you tell me?" Clarissa demanded. "Didn't you tell me that I could ask you anything?"

"Well, yeah, I did," Mike said. "But this is kind of different, sweetheart."

"Why?" Clarissa asked.

Deciding it was time to rescue Mike, Mary pushed the door open and let herself into the bedroom. "Hi sweetie," she said, going over to the bed and giving Clarissa a hug. "How was your day?"

Clarissa hugged her back. "It was great," she said. "Dad and I had a great meeting, and then we ate dinner at This Is It Eatery. And I got deep fried cookies and ice cream for dessert."

"Wow," Mary replied, sitting back and enjoying the excited look on her daughter's face. "That sounds amazing."

Clarissa nodded. "And then we went to the library, and Dad let me take out five new books."

"Well, that's great," Mary said.

"And I signed up for a summer reading program," Clarissa continued. "I can win a prize if I read enough books this summer."

"I think that's awesome," Mary said. "Reading was one of my favorite summertime activities. You can have a new adventure every day."

"Yes, and I even got a book about babies," she said, reaching over and pulling out a slim hardcover book from a pile of books on her nightstand. She handed the book to Mary. "See."

Mary opened the book and flipped through the pages. There were pictures of babies inside their mothers' wombs at different stages of development. "This is really cool," Mary said, looking at a photo that represented the development of her baby at twenty-two weeks. "This is the size of our baby."

Clarissa scooted over and looked at the book. "It's so tiny," she said.

Mary nodded, looking at the information below the photo. "It says that the baby is only eleven inches long and is able to hear sounds now," she said.

"The baby can hear me?" Clarissa asked, her eyes wide with wonder. "Can I talk to the baby?"

"Sure," Mary replied.

The little girl leaned over and placed her head on Mary's stomach. "Hi. I'm your big sister," she said. "My name is Clarissa, and when you are born, we're going to be friends."

Mary felt tears welling in her eyes as she looked down at Clarissa snuggled against her. She placed her hand on the child's head and gently stroked her hair. "I'm sure the baby can't wait to meet you," she whispered.

"Mary, I asked Mike, but he wouldn't tell me," she said. "How do babies get inside your body?"

"That's easy," Mary said, sending Mike a smile. "Love puts them in there."

"Oh," Clarissa replied. "That's nice."

Mary pulled Clarissa into her arms and hugged her. "Yes, that's really nice," she said, cuddling the little girl. "And now you have to go to sleep because you've got a busy day playing with Maggie tomorrow."

Clarissa yawned widely. "Okay, I guess I am kind of tired," she admitted.

"Yeah, me too," Mary agreed, guiding Clarissa onto her pillow. "So, you go to sleep, and I'll go to sleep. And then tomorrow we can wake up and have a great breakfast."

Snuggling deeper into her blankets, Clarissa yawned again. "That's a great idea," she said sleepily. "And know what?"

"What?" Mary asked, standing up and tucking the little girl in.

"We could have waffles for breakfast," she said.

"I think waffles for breakfast is a great idea," Mary agreed. "With strawberries and whipped cream."

Clarissa turned from her pillow, looked up at Mary and smiled. "That would be the best breakfast ever."

Mary leaned over and kissed Clarissa on her forehead. "Then we should definitely have waffles. Good night, sweetheart. I love you."

"Good night, Mary," Clarissa replied, her voice heavy with sleep. "I love you, too."

Mary switched off the light and closed the door behind her. Mike met her in the hallway. "You handled her question really well," he said. "I had no idea what to say."

Mary shrugged. "Well, I have a feeling that the same conversation is going to have a different set of answers in a couple of years," she said as she walked down the hall towards her bedroom.

"Yeah, well, good luck with that," Mike said. Then he looked down at her. "So, how are you feeling?"

"Actually, I'm feeling better," she said. "Although a nice warm bath sounds like heaven."

"Okay, I'll let you go," he said, starting to fade away. "Are you sure you don't need anything?"

"I'm good, but thanks for worrying, Mike," she said with a smile.

"Hey, I'm real good at worrying," he replied, and then he slipped from view. "Especially about people I love."

Chapter Seven

Mary woke up and reached for her phone lying on the nightstand to check the time. It was 2:30 in the morning and, as usual, she had to go to the bathroom. She started to slide out of the covers when she glanced at the end of her bed and froze. The ghost she had met on the street in Galena was sitting at the end of her bed.

"You can see me?" he asked, repeating his question from earlier.

Mary nodded, trying not to wake Bradley who was sleeping beside her. "Yes," she whispered. "I can see you."

"I'm down there," he said. "I can't remember what happened. But I'm down there."

"Down where?" Mary asked. "Where are you?"

"It's dark and quiet, too quiet," he said, his voice dropping to a whisper. "They can't hear me. No one can hear me. I've yelled and screamed, but no one hears me."

"What's your name?" Mary asked.

The ghost paused for a moment, searching for the answer to the question. "I remember," he said slowly, "someone calling me Steve. I think my name is Steve."

"Do you remember your last name?"

He paused again, and after a few silent moments, shook his head. His face held even more anguish than before. "No," he said, his voice breaking with emotion. "I can't remember my last name."

"That's okay, Steve," Mary reassured him. "That's really a normal occurrence."

"Normal occurrence?" he asked, clearly confused. "Normal for what?"

Later, Mary would look back at the moment she answered Steve's question and blame her quick response on the fact that her bladder was near to exploding. "Normal for when you're dead," she replied.

His eyes widened, and his lips quivered with emotion. "I'm dead?" he asked, horrified. "I died?"

Biting her lower lip with regret, she slowly nodded her head. "I'm so sorry, Steve," she said. "I should have handled that in a different way. But, yes, you are dead."

He shook his head. "No, I can't be dead," he argued, his voice raised in anger. "I'm a dad. I have responsibilities. My kids need me. I need to be alive."

Mary just waited for him to finish, silently praying he would hurry.

Suddenly he stopped and stared at her. "You're lying to me," he screamed. "You're a liar. I'm getting out of here. You're nothing but a liar."

"Wait, Steve," Mary called. But he disappeared, and she was left staring into the darkened room.

"Mary? Mary? Are you okay?" Bradley murmured, half-awake.

She placed her hand on his arm to reassure him. "Yes, I'm fine," she whispered. "I just have to go to the bathroom."

"Oh, okay," he muttered, then turned on his side and went back to sleep.

She got up and walked over to the bathroom, regretting her thoughtless words. A few minutes later, she carefully let herself out of her bedroom, closing the door carefully so she didn't wake Bradley. She turned into the hall and nearly ran into Mike.

"I heard," he said without any explanation.

She sighed and leaned against the wall. "So, you know that I was totally self-absorbed and didn't even think that I was giving him the worst news of his entire life."

"No, I saw a woman who took the time, even though she was uncomfortable, to speak with someone in pain," he replied.

Shaking her head, she wiped the tears filling her eyes. "No, Mike, you're just being nice to me," she said. "I was thoughtless and abrupt. I know better than that."

"Unlike me, you're human," he said with a gentle smile. "And you get to make mistakes. Of course, as you probably guessed, even as a human I didn't make mistakes."

She rewarded him with a watery chuckle. "Mike, you can't believe everything your mom used to tell you," she responded automatically.

"See, there's my Mary back in fighting form," he said with a laugh. "So, what do you say we go downstairs and grab some milk and cookies? Bradley forgot to mention that he picked up several of your favorite kinds today."

"Mike, as much as I'd like to believe it, cookies do not solve the problems of the world."

"Yeah, I know," he admitted. "But they sure help when the going gets rough."

Pausing for a moment, undecided, she weighed her options. She really should go back to bed just in case Steve decided to come back. Of course, it was highly unlikely that Steve would come back that night, or any night, she recalled sadly. Then her stomach growled, and she realized she had only eaten a protein bar for dinner. And really, cookies and milk sounded really good. She turned to Mike. "What kind of cookies?" she finally asked.

Grinning, he floated towards the stairs and nodded towards the kitchen. "Why don't we both go downstairs and find out," he suggested.

She pushed up from the wall and shrugged. "Sure, why not?"

By the time she reached the kitchen, Mike already had a glass of milk poured for her and was pulling containers of cookies from the pantry. He looked over his shoulder and motioned with a box of cookies. "Have a seat at the table," he directed. "I'm almost done here."

She looked over to the counter to see a stack of six different containers of cookies. "Mike, I only want one or two of them," she said.

He turned and placed the final two containers on the top of the stack and carried them to the table. "Sure, one or two of each kind," he said. "Mary, you have to remember. You're eating for two."

"Mike, I'm having a baby, not a litter," she complained.

Placing the assortment in front of her, he glided into the chair next to her and then rested his chin on his hands. "Come on, Mary," he coaxed. "Tell Uncle Mike what's wrong."

Ripping open a package of sandwich cookies, she pulled one out and bit down ferociously. "Mike, this isn't funny," she exclaimed as she chewed.

"I didn't say it was," he replied, leaning closer. "Have you always felt that you had to be perfect?"

"I'm not perfect," she replied. "I never said I was perfect."

She absently pulled out another cookie and bit into it. "I just said that I was wrong to tell Steve that he was dead."

"Was he?" Mike asked.

"Was he what?" she asked.

"Was he dead?"

"He's a ghost. Of course he's dead."

"So, you didn't lie, right?

She sat back in her chair and shook her head. "No, I didn't lie," she acknowledged. "But I wasn't careful with his feelings."

"Come on, Mary," he coaxed. "Tell me what's really wrong?"

She picked out another cookie, toyed with it for a few moments and finally nibbled on the edge. "I wanted him to go away," she confessed softly.

Mike lifted an eyebrow. "Say what?"

"I wanted him to go away," she repeated, not meeting his eyes. "I just wanted to be able to get up, go to the bathroom and go back to bed without someone hanging around telling me about their problems."

"Damn Mary, you really aren't perfect," he said.

She slammed the cookie onto the table, breaking it into a dozen smaller pieces. "Well, thanks," she snapped. "I guess not everyone can be an angel."

When Mike chuckled, she reached for an unopened bag of cookies to whip it at his head.

"You know the cookies will fly right through me," Mike said calmly before she could send them in his direction.

She paused, looked at the cookies in her hand, sighed and put them back on the table. "You're right," she muttered, reaching for another cookie. "Why are you always right?"

"Yeah, you don't want me to answer that," he said. "It will just make you angrier. Besides, I was just teasing you. You know I think you're absolutely perfect, and cute too."

His flattery did nothing to improve her mood. This time she placed her chin in her hands and sighed again. "I'm such a terrible person," she whimpered. "I mean, he's dead and he's stuck somewhere, and all I can think about is going to the bathroom. What does that make me?"

"A totally exhausted, pregnant woman who needs a good night's sleep," Mike said. Then reaching over, he placed his hand on her shoulder. "And a woman who is trying to be brave even when her heart is breaking over a little girl who was abused and murdered."

A tear slipped down Mary's cheek. "It was like Clarissa was standing in front of me," she whispered. "If we hadn't found Clarissa, it could have been her."

"But it wasn't Clarissa," he reminded her. "And there is nothing you can do to change that little girl's life. But you can help her by finding out what's keeping here her and then helping her move on. That's your job, not fixing all the ills of the world."

Folding her arms, she laid her head on the table. "I know," she said. "But this time, I wish there was some way to change things."

"Mary, once you help her cross over, you have changed things," he reminded her. "She gets to go home and be surrounded with love."

She nodded slowly and yawned. "You're right."

"And, I think it's time we change the rules again," he said.

Lifting her head, she looked up at him. "Change the rules?"

"Yeah, I think we need to keep your bedroom off limits for a little while," he said. "At least until after the baby is born. You need more sleep."

"Really?" she asked, her voice tinged with excitement. "You think we could change that?"

He smiled at her. "Yeah, I'm pretty sure we can make that change," he said. "So, why don't you go to bed, and I'll get things arranged."

Pushing herself up from her chair, she looked down at him. "Thank you," she said. "You are the best friend I've ever had."

"I feel the same way about you," he replied. "Now go to bed and let Uncle Mike take care of things here."

Chapter Eight

When Mary and Clarissa walked down the street the next morning, they were surprised to find the entire Brennan family standing out on their front porch waiting for them. Mary was so grateful that Katie had agreed to let Clarissa spend most of her summer vacation days with the Brennan family while she and Bradley worked. Maggie and Clarissa had been inseparable most days, and they had split sleepovers between the two houses.

"Hi," Mary called. "What's up?"

"So?" Katie asked.

"So?" Mary repeated, confused.

"I thought your ultrasound was yesterday," Katie replied.

"Yeah, when you get to find out if you're going to have a cool boy baby or a lame girl baby," Andy added.

"Andrew Brennan," Katie reprimanded. "There are no lame babies, boy or girl. They are all a gift from God."

"Yes, Mom," he replied, but then he turned to Mary. "But a boy baby would be awesome."

"Well, the ultrasound is actually this morning," she said, placing her hand on the small mound at her abdomen. "So, if the baby cooperates, we will know who's in there."

"Then we have the party, right?" Maggie asked.

Mary nodded. "Yes, dinner and cupcakes at our house Friday night," she said. "And then we'll make the announcement."

"Wow, Clarissa," Andy said. "You're going to find out if you're going to be a big brother or a big sister."

David, Andy's older brother, cuffed him on the top of his head. "You dork," he laughed. "She's going to be a big sister no matter what."

"David Brennan," Katie said with a long-suffering sigh. "You don't hit your brother."

"Yes, ma'am," David replied, and although the tone of his voice was chastened, the twinkle in his eye demonstrated a wholly unrepentant attitude.

Katie gave David the "mom" look, letting him know that she wasn't fooled before she turned to Mary. "What can I bring?" she asked.

Shaking her head, Mary smiled at her. "Nothing at all," she said. "It's taken care of. Bradley is going to man the grill, and Rosie insisted on making everything else."

"Well, that was sweet of her," Katie said.

Mary nodded. "Yes, it was. And she couldn't stand having to wait to find out who the baby is going to be," she added with a laugh. "So, right after we call my parents, we call Rosie so she can fill the cupcakes with the right color filling."

"Ah, clever lady," Katie said. "And I've tasted Rosie's cooking, so you're pretty clever yourself."

"No matter what, I win," Mary agreed. "So, I'll be back here to pick up Clarissa at about 3:00 this afternoon. Does that work?"

"Perfect," Katie said. "And if she needs to stay later, just let me know. She is absolutely no trouble."

"Thanks," Mary replied. Then she turned and gave Clarissa a hug. "Have a great day, sweetheart."

Clarissa hugged her back. "You, too," she said. "I can't wait to find out."

"Me, too," Mary said.

Walking back to her house, Mary could still hear the discussion about babies and parties coming from the Brennan porch. Andy and David were arguing, and Maggie and Clarissa were guessing what sex the baby would be. Katie stood in the midst and ushered them all inside before "they woke the entire neighborhood and the dead." Mary smiled widely. Katie Brennan was amazing.

Bradley met her at the front door, and she tiptoed to press a kiss on his lips. "Ready?" she asked.

He nodded, but the smile on his face didn't reach his eyes.

"What's wrong?" she asked.

He shook his head. "Nothing," he said. "I'm good. Let's go."

She put her hand on his chest and stopped him as he tried to exit the house. "What's wrong?" she asked again.

Exhaling slowly, he closed his eyes for a moment. "I'm nervous, that's all," he said.

"Nervous?" she asked. "About an ultrasound?"

He chuckled nervously. "Yeah, pretty silly, right?"

She wrapped her arms around his neck and met his eyes. "I'm not Jeannine," she said. "Nothing is going to happen to me or our baby."

His jaw tensed for a moment, and he looked away from her but not before she saw the pain in his eyes. "I keep remembering," he whispered, "how happy we were, how carefree we were. We had no idea that something would change our lives the very next day."

"And you keep waiting for the other shoe to drop," Mary said.

He nodded. "Yeah, I guess I do."

"Well, let me tell you something, Bradley Alden," she said, her voice confident and strong. "This little baby is already a miracle child. So don't you think for a moment that I would let anyone endanger either of us."

He pulled her into his arms and just held her for a moment, not saying a word. "I can't lose you," he finally said.

She wrapped her arms around him and laid her head against his chest. "You won't," she said. "You're stuck with me forever."

"Forever sounds good," he said, kissing her on the top of the head.

"Yeah, well just remember that if the doctor tells us we're having triplets," she replied.

He stepped back, his eyes wide, and his jaw dropped. "There's a chance of that?" he stammered.

She grinned. "Probably not," she said. "But it sure got your mind off other things, didn't it?"

Chapter Nine

Mary hung up the phone, sat back in the chair next to her desk and smiled. She was going to make her mom and dad grandparents again, and it seemed they were even more excited than she and Bradley. When she told them the results of the ultrasound, her mother declared that she could finally start shopping for the baby, and she could hear the tears in her father's voice. She felt her own eyes moisten with tears as she pictured her rugged dad with reddened eyes.

"Another O'Reilly born into the world," he had whispered.

"Timothy O'Reilly," her mother had replied. "The baby will be an Alden, not an O'Reilly."

"Aye, Alden will be the last name," he had countered. "But O'Reilly blood will out. The babe will be an O'Reilly through and through."

Wiping a stray tear away, she took a deep breath and reached for her mouse. But before she could even right click, her office door sprung open, and Rosie and Stanley hurried inside.

"Well?" Stanley said. "You can't keep us waiting any longer. Some of us is older than others. What'cha gonna have?"

Mary shook her head. "But Stanley, it's a secret until Friday," Mary said, holding back a grin. "I promised Bradley that I would only tell my parents and Rosie. Everyone else has to wait until Friday."

"I ain't everyone else," Stanley grumbled. "Well, I'm practically your father."

Rosie giggled. "I'm sure Mary's mother would be surprised by that remark," she said.

"That's not what I meant," he said. "But I've been here through her ups and downs. Why, I even let her borrow my car, and believe you me, that's not something I do lightly."

"But Stanley, I made a promise," Mary said. "And, being the kind of person you are, you wouldn't want me going against my promise, would you?"

"Bah, it ain't breaking a promise iffen you don't say it out loud," he said. "You could just write it down and hand it to Rosie and iffen I happen to see it, well, that's out of your control."

"You don't think that would be lying, do you?" she asked with a smile.

"I'm just saying, you wouldn't be telling me," he replied. "I'd be finding out on my own. Kind of like an act of God."

"I don't think God has any part of this," Rosie said. "Now Stanley, leave Mary alone."

Mary grinned and picked up a folded piece of paper from her desk. She handed it to Rosie and winked at Stanley. "Unfortunately Rosie, Stanley has been a bad influence on me," she said. "I thought of the same thing before you even walked through the door."

"Oh. Oh. Oh," Rosie squealed as she unwrapped the note. "Oh, it's a—"

"Shhhh!" Mary said, stopping Rosie before she uttered the last word. "We don't want to have to tell Bradley that you told Stanley."

Stanley scooted behind Rosie's shoulder and read what was printed on the note and nodded at Mary, his eyes warm with happiness. "Well, congratulations to the two of you," he said. "I couldn't be prouder iffen you were my own daughter."

Mary got up, walked around her desk and gave Stanley a kiss on the cheek. "Thank you, Stanley," she said.

Then she turned and hugged Rosie. "And thank you for helping with the party."

Rosie's eyes were brimming with tears. "Oh, Mary, I'm just so happy for you," she said. "Are you going to tell Clarissa tonight?"

"We asked Clarissa if she wanted to know tonight or if she wanted to wait until Friday," Mary explained. "And she actually chose waiting until Friday."

"She did?" Rosie exclaimed. "Why would she do that?"

"Well, she knew that it would be too hard to keep the secret between now and then," Mary said with a smile. "And she didn't want to be the one to spill the beans."

"Smart girl," Stanley said. "Besides, it will be more fun when everyone finds out at the same time."

Rosie lifted an eyebrow in his direction. "Oh really?" she asked.

With an embarrassed chuckle, he shrugged. "Well, fun for everyone but me."

Rosie turned back to Mary and shook her head. "He's incorrigible."

Mary laughed. "That's okay," she said. "We like him just the way he is."

"Good thing for him," Rosie added. Then she pulled a list from her purse. "So, how many people should I plan for?"

"Well, my parents will be there, all three of my brothers, the entire Brennan family," Mary listed.

"And when Ian heard you'd be cooking, he insisted on coming with Gillian."

Rosie blushed slightly. "Isn't that sweet of him."

"Bradley is going to call Jeannine's parents and see if they would like to come," Mary continued.

"That's awfully nice of him," Stanley said.

"Well, they're Clarissa's grandparents," Mary said. "So, we think they should be part of the new baby's life, too, if they want to be."

Rosie looked over her shoulder and then lowered her voice. "I've never asked. And really, it's none of my business," she began.

"But that ain't never stopped her before," Stanley inserted.

She frowned at Stanley for a moment and then turned back to Mary. "Where are Bradley's parents?" she asked. "He never talks about them."

"They passed away when he was in the service," Mary explained. "They were in a car accident when he was deployed. So, really, the only parents he's had for years were Jeannine's mom and dad."

"Oh, dear, well no wonder he wants to invite them," Rosie said. "I really hope they come."

Nodding, Mary smiled at her. "Me, too," she said. "We want to share the news with everyone we love."

Rosie put the list back into her purse. "Well, it's going to be a great party," Rosie said, and then she turned to look at Stanley, "as long as no one lets the cat out of the bag."

"Don't look at me," Stanley grumbled. "My lips are sealed. No one is going to hear from me that Mary is going to have a baby—"

"Stanley!" both women yelled.

Chuckling softly, Stanley winked at the women. "Just kidding."

Chapter Ten

Mary opened the small, plastic container and took two boiled eggs from it and placed them on the paper plate on top of her small office refrigerator. Putting the lid back on the container, she snapped it closed and put it back on the refrigerator shelf and closed the door. Picking up the small, glass, pepper shaker, she started to sprinkle pepper on the eggs.

"Hey, Mary, what's up?" Mike asked as he suddenly appeared next to her.

Startled, Mary swung around, hurtling the pepper shaker through the air where it crashed into a mirror hanging on the wall and caused it to shatter.

They both stared at the broken mirror for a moment. Finally, Mike rocked back on his heels and cleared his throat cautiously. "So, how's that bad luck horoscope working for you so far?" he asked.

She glared at him for a moment. "Well, I was doing pretty well until a certain someone just made me break a mirror," she replied. "I believe that's seven years bad luck if I'm not mistaken."

"Mary, you can't believe in those old superstitions," Mike said. "They were created back in a day when people were ignorant of true science, when they would believe in anything."

"Like ghosts and angels?" Mary countered.

"Touché," Mike replied.

Sighing, Mary picked up a roll of paper towels and her trash can. "Well, I might as well clean it up," she said, walking across the room to the mess.

She had just bent over to pick up the first large shard of mirror when her phone rang. Standing, she hurried over to her desk and answered. "Mary O'Reilly."

"Hello, Mary, this is Donna from Galena," the voice on the other end stated. "She came back. She's here right now, and we want to be sure we ask her the right questions."

Mary slipped into her chair and pulled out a pen and paper pad. "That's great, Donna," she said. "Can you ask her for her full name?"

She could hear Donna relaying the information to her son, Ryan, and Ryan asking Liza.

"Her name is Liza Parker," Ryan said.

"Does she know how old she is?" Mary asked.

Donna repeated the question to Ryan.

"She's five, but her birthday is in September and she will be six," Ryan said brightly.

Mary's heart ached for the little girl who would never see her sixth birthday. "Ask her if she knows her address," Mary said.

Donna repeated the question and Mary heard Ryan ask it. There was a long pause while Ryan waited for the response. "She doesn't know her newest address," he said. "She didn't live there for very long. That's where the bad man lives. But she used to live with her first family in a place called Dubuque."

"Does she remember the name of her first family?" Mary asked.

"She said she remembers their last name was Larson," Ryan said, "because they called her Liza Larson for a little while."

"Does she remember what year she lived with the Larsons?" Mary asked, crossing her fingers.

Donna relayed the question to Ryan, and Mary could hear Ryan asking Liza.

"She's getting tired," Ryan said. "She really doesn't want to answer any more questions. They make her sad."

"If she could just answer this one, it would be so helpful," Mary pleaded.

She heard Donna ask Ryan one more time.

"She says that she remembers a New Year's Eve Party with the Larsons just before the mom got sick," Ryan said. "And it was for 2010. Does that help?"

"It helps a lot," Mary replied. "Thank you so much. Please tell Liza that she's done a wonderful job today."

"Is there anything else I should do?" Donna asked.

"If Ryan tells you anything else, please call me," Mary said. "But you have both been amazing. I'm sure there's going to be information about a missing girl out there, and this will help me narrow down the search."

"Okay, I'll write anything down that Ryan tells me," she replied. "Thank you for helping us, Mary."

"Thank you for helping Liza," Mary replied.

After hanging up the phone, she smiled at Mike, who was busy cleaning up mirror shards. "Well, this should be a piece of cake," she replied. "There's got to be a record of this little girl out there somewhere."

Chapter Eleven

Mary sat at a small desk in the corner of Bradley's office typing on the keyboard connected to a dedicated computer system that accessed the law enforcement databases available to the Freeport Police department. Finally, she sighed with frustration. "I can't believe there is no record out there," Mary said, pushing herself away from the desk and computer screen. "A child doesn't simply disappear and have no one report her. Someone has to know."

Bradley looked up from the reports he was filling out at his desk. "No missing persons report?" he asked.

She shook her head. "No missing persons, no hospital reports, no DCFS reports," she said. "It's like she never existed."

He leaned back in his chair and tucked his hands behind his head, contemplating the situation for a moment. Finally, he sat forward and met Mary's eyes. "A couple of months ago, I received a memo about a situation in Wisconsin where a child was re-homed."

Mary shook her head. "Re-homed? What's that?"

"It's basically a practice where someone puts an adopted child up for adoption again," Bradley said. "But the adoptive parents use social networking to find new parents; they don't go through an agency."

"Wait. They give their child away like you would give away a puppy?" Mary asked, shocked.

Nodding, Bradley reached over and typed on his keyboard. "Yeah, it's generally done with older kids, and very often they have been international adoptions," he said. "The parents find they can't handle the child's behavior, or circumstances in their lives change. So they look for another home for the child. In the Wisconsin case, the couple who adopted the child turned out to be child molesters. Luckily for the child, the first set of parents decided to check up on the child. It was only when they couldn't get in touch with the new parents that they called the police and found out the new parents had not only falsified their information but their own children had also been taken away from them because they had violent tendencies."

"So, there's no official record, no documentation for these children that have been re-homed?" Mary asked.

Bradley shook his head. "No, and according to the reading I did, there have been at least 5000 cases of re-homing in the past five years."

"Liza did mention that her family gave her away to someone else," Mary said. "I wonder if that's the reason there's no record."

"That makes sense to me," Bradley agreed.

"Okay, first I have to get my head around the fact that people would think it's okay to give away a child," she said, sitting back in her chair, "to people they don't know with no background checks, no governmental knowledge, and no safety net for the child."

"Not that this is a justification," Bradley said, "but many of the cases of re-homing were with older children who had behavioral problems. The parents just couldn't handle them, so they looked for other families who were more capable of dealing with things like that."

"But isn't adoption kind of like marriage?" Mary asked. "For better or for worse, in sickness and in health? When the going gets tough, you don't just give a child away."

"No, you're right," he agreed. "You don't give up when the going gets tough."

Sighing in frustration, Mary picked up her pad of paper and scanned her notes. "Well, this adds a whole different layer to the investigation."

"But if she was re-homed, and she was killed by the new parents, it adds more urgency to the case," Bradley said, "because people are still re-homing their children through the Internet."

"Liza said that she lived in Dubuque with her first family," Mary said. "I would think the first adoption was done legally. Do you think you could make an official call to the courthouse in Dubuque and see if you could gain access to her adoption records?"

Bradley picked up the phone and pressed a button. "Hi, Dorothy," he said. "Could you get me the Dubuque County Courthouse in Dubuque, Iowa? I need to talk to someone about adoption records and a possible abuse case."

He hung up the phone. "Now we just wait and see how cooperative they are going to be. Generally, especially in cases of child abuse, they will open the closed adoption files."

"Well, if that doesn't work, I'll be calling every family with the last name of Larson in Dubuque County to find out if they ever adopted a little girl," Mary said. "This is really frightening, Bradley. That little girl was brutally murdered, and the man who did it to her might be gaining access to other children the same way."

Chapter Twelve

Joseph Amoretti pushed open the doors of the gentlemen's club and squinted into the bright sunlight. He was a dapper man with an olive complexion, a neatly groomed moustache and dark, thick hair. Dressed casually in designer jeans and a button down shirt, the lifts stuffed inside his leather shoes gave a few more inches to his five-foot five-inch height. He took a deep breath, inhaling the unique scent of the Mississippi River only a hundred feet away. The East Dubuque Strip lay along the riverbank, littered with nightclubs, gentlemen's clubs and bars. And Joey felt perfectly at home in the area reminiscent of the Illinois town's darker history.

He paused in front of his car and checked out his reflection, running his fingers through his hair to give it the tousled, sexy look he felt flattered his face. Opening the car door, he reached in and pulled out a bottle of mouthwash. The few drinks he had allowed himself were just a little treat before he had another busy day, but he didn't want his wife, Gigi, to notice them on his breath. Taking a swig of the mint-flavored liquid, he swished it around for a minute before spiting it out on the gravel parking lot.

After opening his car door, he pulled out his wallet, thick with bills, and congratulated himself on another job well done. It hadn't taken him very long to turn this transaction into profit. She'd only been with him for four months. It was just enough time to present the façade of respectability and reassure the family who had given her up. And she was a beauty, he sighed, shaking his head. If his wife wasn't so damn crazy, he might have considered keeping the girl around.

With a slight shrug, he slid his light frame behind the wheel of his car and headed home. He needed to shower, shave and change into his vestments to meet the newest member of his family. He glanced into the rearview mirror and noted his bloodshot eyes. "Yeah, the good reverend is going to have to use some eye drops to make himself presentable," he sneered. "Don't want to screw up the deal."

Driving away from the Mississippi river, he continued up the winding roads that led away from downtown East Dubuque into the solitude of the countryside. Considering himself an expert in crime throughout history, he smirked as he passed through quiet, residential neighborhoods and picturesque parks. "All dressed up and looking respectable," he muttered, "when you know you ain't any better than me. Ain't nothing but window dressing."

In its heyday, East Dubuque was known as "Sin City" for its speakeasies, nightclubs, whiskey stills hidden in the hills during Prohibition, and its connection with the notorious mobster, Al Capone.

"There's always a market for sin," Joey said, thinking about the money in his wallet.

He drove south beyond the town limits into the countryside. These roads, the same ones the bootleggers used nearly a hundred years ago, wove through thick, forested woods and farmlands to isolated destinations that were perfect for concealing all kinds of nefarious actions.

Finally, after about twenty minutes, he pulled up on the dirt road in front of the dilapidated farmhouse and parked his car. Before he exited the car, the front door of the house opened and a petite middle-aged woman met him. She was dressed in a modest skirt and blouse, her hair carefully coiffed. She wore pearls around her neck and on studs through her earlobes. She looked decisively like a minister's wife until you looked into her eyes.

Angelina Gambino Amoretti, or Gigi as her daddy always called her, was the daughter of one of the top crime bosses in Chicago. She was a real looker, curves in all the right places, blonde hair that glimmered in the light, and a mouth that was so plump and ripe it took all he had not to taste it the first time he met her. Yeah, he thought, grabbing his wallet from the dashboard, and see where that got me.

"How did it go?" Gigi asked.

He reached in his wallet and pulled out the stack of hundred dollar bills. "We hit the jackpot," he said, placing a kiss on her cheek. "And she was worth every cent."

She snatched the bills from his hand, placed them inside her handbag and then looked him over. "You look and smell disgusting," she said. "Go in and clean up, and be quick about it. We've got to drive down to Clinton to meet this new family."

"Yeah, I'm going," he grumbled.

"And this time, don't forget to bring your holy books," she called after him. "What kind of minister are you without a Bible?"

He stopped on the first step of the porch and turned back to her. "The kind that gets his rewards here on earth, my dear," he sneered, grabbing his crotch and smiling, "and enjoys the blessings of the flesh."

"Yes, I noticed," she said, glaring at him with such venom that he nearly stumbled. "In the future, just remember that I give you the ones you can sample. The other ones, you keep your hands off."

He shrugged. "Just breaking them in, my dear," he replied carefully. "They don't mean nothing to me. None of them are as sexy as you are."

Her eyes softened for a moment, and then she shook her head. "Don't try to sweet-talk me, you Casanova. You don't touch them unless I say so," she repeated. "Do you understand?"

Nodding, he stepped back toward the door. "Yeah. I do," he said.

"Good," she said, meeting his eyes. "Because I can dig a big hole in the forest just as well as I can dig a small one."

A chill ran down his spine as he considered the collection of graves behind their barn. "I won't touch one ever again, Gigi," he breathed. "I promise."

Chapter Thirteen

"Where are you going?" Mike asked, appearing in front of Mary as she headed out of her office door.

She stopped suddenly, her hand on her chest, and took a deep breath. "You really have to stop doing that," she said pointedly. "This can't be good for the baby."

Mike looked ashamed. "Sorry," he said.

"Really. I'm sorry," he repeated when she gave him a skeptical look. "I was just going to check in on you, and suddenly, you're going out the door. Does Bradley know?"

Sighing audibly, Mary put her hands on her hips and met Mike's eyes. "I am going to Galena," she said. "I need to see if I can find out any more information about Steve. Bradley does know that I'm going, but not because I have to ask his permission to do my job. He knows because we both let each other know what we are doing. I'm fine. I'm healthy. And I can drive my car."

"Yeah, yeah, I know you can," Mike said. "It's just...well, Mary, you're pregnant. And I've never gone through pregnancy before."

"And you're not going through pregnancy now," Mary replied.

"Well, yeah, okay, if you want to be technical," he said, feeling hurt. "I just don't know how to protect you."

She slowly shook her head. "Mike, is that your assignment? To protect me?" she asked. "Or are you just getting a little carried away here?"

"Well, I get to watch over you now, too," he said. "Because of the baby."

"Well then, I don't mind you watching over me, and I don't mind your company," she said. "But could you just calm down a little? You're making me nervous."

"Sorry," he said. "I'll try to be calmer."

He slid out of the way so she could open the door, but then she stopped and looked outside. A light summer rain had begun to fall. Reaching over to the coat rack near the door, she grabbed an umbrella and started to open it.

"Mary! Stop!" he yelled.

She froze. "What?" she demanded.

"You nearly opened an umbrella inside," he said. "That's bad luck."

She looked at him and then looked at the umbrella. "You're right," she said. "I forgot."

She stepped up to the door, held the umbrella outside and then opened it. "Thanks, Mike," she replied. "I certainly don't need any more bad luck coming my way."

She walked to her car with Mike following alongside. "So what are we doing in Galena today?" he asked.

"We?" she replied, lifting an eyebrow.

"You said you didn't mind my company," he said with a charming smile.

Laughing, she shook her head as she entered the car. "Well, we are going to stop at Amelia's and see if she can shed any light on what could have happened to Steve."

"Well, that ought to be fun," Mike said. "And I suppose I should stay outside?"

"Well, you can come in," Mary agreed, putting the key in the car and turning on the engine. "But if she starts coughing, you need to leave."

"That's weird that her response to the paranormal is to get choked up," he said as they pulled out of their parking spot.

Mary shrugged. "Makes you kind of wonder how many other people have the same response but don't realize it's because of a ghost."

Mike grinned and then coughed. "Allergies," he said with another mock cough. "Strangest thing, they just show up every so often."

Mary raised her eyebrows and grinned. "Perhaps you're allergic to ghosts," she said in a quietly spooky voice.

"Yeah, I can just hear a doctor give that as a diagnosis," Mike said.

"Dr. Frankenstein, maybe," Mary teased.

The turned onto Highway 20 and headed west toward Galena. The rain had stopped, but a beautiful rainbow glittered in the sky. Mary glanced up at it and smiled. "I've always felt that rainbows were reminders from God," she said.

"Really? Reminders of what?" Mike asked.

"Reminders that no matter how bad the storm is, there is always something beautiful and wondrous on the other side," she said. "You just have to look for it."

"Why, Mary Alden, you're a poet," Mike teased.

"No, I'm just someone who's been through a lot of storms," she said. "And I have always found a rainbow on the other side."

"Do you think everyone gets a rainbow?" he asked.

She nodded slowly as she thought about her answer. "Yes, actually I do," she said. "But if you're looking down, you'll miss it."

"What's Liza's rainbow?" he asked quietly.

"She'll never be hurt again," Mary replied sadly, and then she smiled softly. "And she found Donna and Ryan."

"Have you found out anything about her yet?" he asked.

"Bradley is trying to get her adoption records open," Mary said. "He's making some calls to Dubuque. That's why I decided to concentrate on Steve. I can't do anything more for Liza right now."

Mike nodded and looked out the window for a moment. "What was my rainbow, Mary?" he finally asked.

Mary glanced over to her friend, saw the sadness in his eyes and wished she had the words to take the sadness away. "I don't know," she replied. "Nothing you did caused your death. It was caused by the actions of someone with a clearly unhinged mind. You were a victim, and your life ended far sooner than it should have."

She slowed the car as they entered one of the small towns on Highway 20 and they passed a schoolyard filled with children. "You would have been a great dad," she said quietly.

He didn't respond at first but watched the children running after each other, laughing with simple pleasure. "You know, all of my life, especially after Timmy died, all I wanted to do was protect people," he said. "That's why I became a firefighter. And even though my life ended too soon, I'm still doing what I wanted to do. I'm protecting the people I love. I guess I did get a rainbow."

She smiled at him. "Well, I know that you're one of my rainbows," she said.

"Yeah, your most charming, sexy and irresistible rainbow," he said with a grin.

"Don't forget modest," Mary added. "You always forget that one."

He laughed out loud. "Yeah, and you always remind me."

Chapter Fourteen

Mary counted her blessings when she found a parking spot right in front of Amelia's shop. The bells above the door jingled as she walked in, and Amelia hurried out of the backroom.

"Oh, Mary. Hi," she said. "It's great to see you back so soon."

"Hi Amelia," Mary said, returning Amelia's smile. "I have another case here in Galena, and I was looking for some information."

"Pull up a chair," Amelia said, "and I'll be happy to give you any information I can."

"Okay, well, this is a weird one," Mary began.

"What's not weird when you and my wife are involved together," Andy, Amelia's husband, said as he walked in from the back room.

Mary smiled at him. "Well, okay, you have an excellent point there," she admitted. "But this one is really different."

Andy pulled up a chair and sat down with them. "Okay, spill it," he said.

"Earlier in the week, when I was here, I saw another ghost," she said. "But when I first saw him, I only saw half of his body."

"Half his body?" Amelia repeated, wrinkling her nose is distaste. "That's disgusting."

"Well, it's not like I saw him chopped in half," Mary amended. "It's like the other half of his body was stuck in the ground, and I could only see him from the waist up. Like he was underground."

Andy shrugged. "Well, that's not too hard to believe considering Galena is filled with old mine shafts and crevices," he said.

"Old mine shafts?" Mary asked.

Nodding, Andy sat forward in his chair. "Yeah, there were a lot of miners who just had small, one-person mines," he said. "They were deep and narrow, just big enough for one person and their equipment. They're all over the place."

"But he's not old enough to be a miner," Mary said. "He's wearing pretty contemporary clothing."

"What's his name?" Amelia asked.

"Steve," Mary said. "But he can't remember his last name."

"What else is significant about him?" Andy asked.

Mary paused. "Well, okay, but this is going to sound really gross," she said.

"Cool," Andy replied.

Laughing, Mary shook her head. "Okay, you asked for it," she said. "It seems to me that a portion of his body was actually decomposing before he died. I don't know how that could happen."

Andy sat back in his chair and crossed one leg over the other. "Well, this might add to the grossness of this conversation," he said. "But because of how hard it was to run city sewer lines to a lot of the houses on the tops of the bluffs or the hills, especially the big houses on streets like Prospect, many of the houses just emptied their sewer lines into the old mine shafts or the crevices in the rock."

"That's really disgusting," Amelia said. "That can't be true."

Shaking his head, Andy looked at his wife. "Disgusting and true," he said. "When I did some construction work, we often ran into some of the old houses that still had their lines just dumping straight down. And occasionally, we'd run into an old mine that had just been covered over with wood boards and sod."

"Boards and sod?" Mary asked, surprised. "But when the wood rots…"

"Yeah, it can be a nasty surprise," Andy agreed.

"How deep were the mines?" Mary asked.

"Sometimes the shafts were forty or fifty feet deep," he said. "They would often have offshoot tunnels where the actual mining went on every twenty feet or so."

"That's really dangerous," Amelia said.

"Well, most of them are filled in now," Andy reassured her. "But since there was no record of where all the mines were located, every so often a new one is located."

"If Steve had fallen down one of the shafts, what are the chances that his remains could be located?" Mary asked.

Andy shrugged. "I guess it depends on how far he fell," he said. "And what he fell into."

"I really didn't want that mental picture," Amelia said.

"Sorry," he apologized.

"Well, this explains a lot," Mary said. "Why his body was in the condition it was in, why he's half in and half out of the ground. Now all I have to do is find out his last name and where he might have lived before he died."

"Missing persons?" Amelia suggested.

Mary nodded. "Yes, I'll try there first," she said, standing up. "Thanks for your help. I'm really glad you were here, Andy."

"Hey, no problem," he replied. "Any friend of Amelia's is a friend of mine."

Chapter Fifteen

The drive from East Dubuque to Clinton Iowa took a little over an hour along the scenic Mississippi River. But the occupants of the car were not interested in the view; they were more concerned with perfecting their story before they met with the adoptive parents of their next transaction. Joey and Gigi Amoretti had found their own private treasure trove in the naïve and desperate parents on an Internet list who had adopted children they could no longer handle. Many of the children had been international adoptions and were older children who had a hard time adapting to their new parents and their new surroundings. Posing as a well-meaning pastor and his compassionate wife, Joey and Gigi sympathized with the overwhelmed parents and offered their home as one of refuge for the struggling youth.

Had any of the parents taken the time to do a background check on the two, they would have found a history of criminal activity from petty theft to embezzlement. They would have learned that the good minister Joseph Amoretti was in reality Little Joey Amoretti with connections to the mob. But, much to the dismay of his parents, Little Joey had been a failure in the organized crime community. Gigi's father saw a way to unload his daughter before she brought too much public notoriety to the family. He made a deal with Joey. Joey took care of Gigi and found her an outlet for her "unique" hobbies, and Daddy made sure they were both taken care of.

Joey moved Gigi out of the city and bought her a farm where he thought she'd be happy. They were working with the family in Chicago moving stolen goods through an Internet site when they happened upon the adoption thread and found, to their amazement, people who were willing to turn over their adopted daughters to strangers.

"Now remember, Joey," Gigi repeated. "We just got back from a mission trip to Haiti, and we discovered how much we loved the people there."

"Don't we need to speak the language?" Joey asked. "What is it Haitianese?"

"No, you idiot," she snapped. "The people of Haiti speak French and Creole. So, we just tell them that we had an interpreter work with us, but we are trying to learn French."

"What if they know French?" he asked. "What do we do then?"

"We tell them we just started the lessons," she said.

"But shouldn't we know something?" he asked. "Like a phrase?"

Rolling her eyes, she sighed loudly. "Yes, we should," she said. "Which is why I gave you that list of French phrases to study last week."

Joey nodded slowly. "Oh, yeah, I remember," he said. "Parsley view Francine."

"That's parlez vous francais?" she huffed and then shook her head. "Maybe we should just say that I'm trying to learn French."

Joey nodded eagerly. "Yeah, because I'm too busy helping folks because I'm a minister and everything," he said.

"Yes, I think that will work," she replied. "Besides, this couple seems so desperate I don't think they are going to question much. Do you have the paper from the social worker?"

"You mean the one you wrote?" he asked.

"Of course I mean the one I wrote," she replied. "Did you print it off using the stolen Illinois State stationery?"

"Yeah, it looks real. Just like a social worker actually came to our house," he laughed. "Damn, this is such a great scam. We take kids off the hands of parents who don't want them, and we put them in the hands of people who *really* want them."

Gigi nodded. "And the fact most of them can't speak English is genius," she said. "We should really try and adopt only foreign ones from now on. American ones get lippy, like that little know-it-all Liza."

Joey shuddered inwardly. He didn't mind the sex or even the violence. It made him feel powerful. But the things Gigi had him do to that little girl while she watched went further than he'd ever gone before. Every time he closed his eyes he could see the look on Gigi's face as he choked the life out of the five-year-old. She had relished every moment of it.

"Yeah, she was a know-it-all," he agreed. "But we took care of her."

Her sudden, uncharacteristic, childlike giggle caused a chill to run down Joey's spine.

"Yes, we did take care of her," she laughed. "We showed her. But next time, Joey…"

He glanced over at her from the driver's seat. "Yes?"

"Next time, I want to help."

They arrived in Clinton and found the local restaurant where the young couple arranged to meet them. Exiting the car, Joey straightened his shirt, adjusting the white collar underneath, and slipped his

73

suit jacket over it. Gigi patted her hair and sent a tender smile in Joey's direction, just in case the couple was watching them. They walked, arm in arm, through the doorway of the restaurant and paused to locate the couple.

Chapter Sixteen

The Galena Police Department was located a few blocks up Main Street from Amelia's storefront. Since the day was lovely and good parking spots were hard to come by, Mary decided to walk up the few blocks to the station. Over 40 years ago, the original town limits, primarily the downtown area, were placed on the National Register of Historic Districts. This meant that those buildings within the boundaries had to look as they did in the mining boomtown days of the 1850s. So any exterior work to a building needed to comply with the Historic Preservation Ordinance. This kept the downtown area of the City of Galena, in Mary's opinion, quaint and cozy. And even though shop windows might advertise the newest offerings in technology or gourmet foods, the ambiance was friendly and welcoming.

Hot summer sun reflected off concrete sidewalks and cobblestoned streets, and Mary felt drops of perspiration on her forehead by the time she'd climbed the three uphill blocks.

"Well, at least the way back will be downhill," she murmured as she crossed the final side street.

"Funny, I haven't had a problem with the walk at all," Mike said, floating next to her.

"Mike," she said. "Shut up."

The offices of the police department were housed in a stately, brick building that Mary thought might have been one of the original city banks. The thick stone and brick façade certainly looked like they were protecting something of value. She stepped up into the doorway and pulled open the heavy, oak door. Immediate relief in the form of very modern air conditioning greeted her, and she made her way to the offices housing the police department. She and Bradley had met Galena's chief of police, a very capable police woman, at a law enforcement function, but Mary decided against asking for personal favors. She'd just as soon ask the clerk for help.

She pushed open the door to the department and waited on the other side of the counter for help. Mike floated through the door and waited next to her. Within moments, a young police officer greeted her.

"Hello, can I help you?" he asked.

Mary nodded. "Yes, thank you. I'm interested in missing persons' files from Galena in the past twenty years," she said. "All I have is a first name and an approximate description to go by."

"Are you related to this person?" the officer asked.

Shaking her head, Mary smiled at the officer. "No, I'm not," she explained. "I've just recently been asked to look into his disappearance, and I really don't have a whole lot to go on."

She pulled out her private investigator's license and showed it to him. He studied it for a moment and then met her eyes. "Aren't you the P.I. who helped with the murder case connected with the former mayor of Freeport last year?" he asked.

"See, he knows you," Mike said. "Obviously he's impressed."

"Yes, that was me," she replied, praying that he hadn't heard about her literal run-in with the fort in Elizabeth.

"There were some pretty crazy rumors circulating about that case," he said, still watching her eyes.

Mike snorted, "Crazy rumors? You? How strange."

"Well, yes, there were, weren't there," she replied easily, steadily returning his gaze and ignoring Mike. "Was there anything you'd like to ask me about those rumors?"

A slow smile spread across his face, and he shook his head. "No, ma'am," he said. "It was damn good investigating no matter how it got done."

Her smile widened. "Why, thank you," she replied.

He turned to his computer and typed on his keyboard, then looked up at her. "The first name?" he asked.

"Steve," she replied with a grateful smile.

"How old do you think he was at the time of his disappearance?"

Mary closed her eyes for a moment, picturing the ghost. "I'd say early to mid-thirties," she finally replied. "And he had a family with small children."

The officer typed the information into the search form. "How tall would you say he was?"

"Close to six feet tall," she said, "with dark blonde hair and hazel eyes."

The officer nodded, keeping his eyes on the screen. "And when did you say he went missing?"

"Well, now, that's the tricky part," she replied, nervously biting her lower lip. "It could have been anytime from the sixties until today."

His fingers stilled on the keyboard, and he looked at her. "Ma'am, that's more than a fifty year time period," he said slowly.

"I think he's getting a little worried," Mike whispered.

She shrugged apologetically. "Yeah, I know," she said. "Sorry I can't be more specific."

He studied her for a moment longer and then turned and entered the information. "Is he deceased?" he asked.

"Yes, but you wouldn't know that," she blurted without thinking.

"Uh oh, bad answer, Mary," Mike said.

Looking up again, he lifted his hands from the keyboard. "Would you like to explain that comment, ma'am?" he asked.

"I'd really rather not," she said honestly. "But if you want me to, I will."

"I won't like it, will I?" he asked.

She shrugged again. "Well, it just depends on whether or not you believe in ghosts," she replied.

"Is honesty the best policy?" Mike wondered aloud. "I guess we're going to find out."

He stared at her a moment longer, thought about it, sighed, and then turned back to his keyboard and entered the information. "Deceased, unknown," he said as he typed.

Keeping an eye on Mary, he surreptitiously slipped his left hand under the counter and pressed a small button mounted on the underside of the counter. Then, in plain sight, he moved the mouse over the search button, clicked and turned to Mary. "Now all we have to do is wait," he said.

Chapter Seventeen

"How long are we going to have to wait?" Joey Amoretti growled softly as he and his wife, Gigi, sat in the run-down diner on the edge of Clinton.

Gigi reached across the table, for all intents and purposes looking like a loving and concerned wife, and placed her hand on top of her husband's. Squeezing tightly and embedding a fingernail into his fleshy palm, she smiled tightly. "People are watching us, sweetheart," she said softly, placing special emphasis on the last word. "We don't want to draw any attention to ourselves."

He returned the smile and endured the pain. "You're right, darling," he replied softly. "I was merely concerned about their safety."

Finally, the door at the far end of the room opened and a young, very flustered looking couple darted into the diner. They scanned the room quickly, and when they saw Joey and Gigi, a glimmer of relief raced across their faces. Hands clasped together, they hurried across the room towards the Amoretti table.

"They didn't bring the kid," Joey whispered through tightened lips. "What the hell?"

"Shhhh, Pastor Amoretti," Gigi warned.

The couple pulled up chairs. "I'm so sorry we're late," the woman explained, her voice breathy. "It's been one of those days."

"Oh my dear, I hope everything is fine," Gigi said, a slight southern accent coloring her words.

The woman nodded. "Yes, we're fine…now," she replied. "We had another issue with Nadia, our daughter. She overheard us discussing her re-homing, and she ran away."

"Ran away?" Joey exclaimed, nearly jumping out of his chair.

"Darling," Gigi said, putting her hand on Joey's arm. "I know you're concerned about the young woman, but I'm sure her parents would not be here with us unless she was safe."

She turned and smiled at the young couple. "He is so concerned about the youth of our country," she explained. "She is fine, isn't she?"

"Yes. Yes, of course," the young man said. "We found her walking towards the bus station. We put her in the car and brought her back home."

Joey clenched his fists under the table, trying to maintain his composure. "But aren't you afraid she'll run again?" he asked, controlling his voice so it merely sounded concerned.

The young woman shook her head. "No, because we promised her that we would postpone our decision to re-home her," she said. "It seems she really does care for us. She just has a difficult time showing her true feelings."

"But we had an agreement," Joey said, his teeth clenched in a smile as he contemplated the loss of income this young woman would have provided. "I was so looking forward to bringing this troubled child into our fold."

"Well, it's just not going to happen," the young man replied, protectively placing his arm around his wife's shoulders. "We came here to let you know that we are going to keep Nadia."

Joey took a deep breath, his face becoming slightly mottled as he tried to contain his anger. "You do realize, young man, that the authorities don't look kindly on people who don't honor their contracts," he said, leaning forward over the table and lowering his voice menacingly. "And DCFS doesn't approve of families who are willing to give their children away."

"Well, I'm sure that if the authorities come and visit us about Nadia, we will be sure to tell them about the good minister and his wife who are willing to take in a number of wayward children," the young man replied, coldly meeting Joey's eyes. "They might want to interview some of those children just to be sure everything is as joyful as you profess."

Joey slowly sat back in his chair, trying not to let the young father see the fear beating in his heart. "I am simply concerned about Nadia," he said, a smile spreading across his face while he nervously smoothed his moustache. "I just want you...both of you...to be sure you still want the responsibility of raising this troubled child."

"Yes. Yes, we do," the young mother said, smiling at Joey. "Thank you for your concern. But we understand now that we just needed to slow down and try to understand each other. And you will be happy to know that if not for your intercession, we would have never had the chance to truly understand our daughter."

"Well, isn't that wonderful, dear," Gigi inserted before Joey could say another word. "It's as if we were sent to you from God to strengthen your little family. And we are so pleased to have been employed as angelic messengers to bless your lives."

The young father rolled his eyes as he sat back in his chair. "Well, bottom line," he said. "We're keeping Nadia. We appreciate your offer, but the deal is off."

"Well, we couldn't be happier," Gigi said, reaching across the table and clasping the young man's hand in both of hers. "I can tell by the light in your eyes that you love your daughter, and truly, that fills our hearts with joy."

Pulling her hands back, she placed her hand on her husband's shoulder and stood up. "Well, we shouldn't be keeping you away from your child any longer," she said. "God Bless You. Come along, dear. Our work here is done."

"Yeah, God Bless you," Joey muttered, getting to his feet. "I hope your family will be very happy."

"We will," the young man said.

Gigi slipped her arm through Joey's and pulled him away from the table before he could reply.

"Little prick," Joey muttered as they walked to the door.

"Shut up, Joey," Gigi whispered sharply. "We've got to get out of the damn parking lot before they think about writing down our license plate and giving that to the cops."

Joey glanced over his shoulder to see the young man watching them with suspicious eyes. "Let's get the hell outta here."

Chapter Eighteen

Mary tried not to tap her fingers on the countertop as she waited for the search engine to come up with results. The young police officer sat calmly at his desk systematically flipping through a stack of mail and placing it in mail slots on the wall.

"I don't have a good feeling about this," Mike said.

"I'm sure we'll be getting an answer in just a minute," the desk officer said as he moved away from her to the back of the room. "The system has been slow lately."

Mary nodded and smiled brightly. "No problem," she said. "I appreciate your help."

The door opened behind her, and Mary was surprised to see two uniformed officers with their guns drawn entering the area.

"Whoa," Mike said. "I guess honesty is not the best policy."

Mary pressed her back against the counter, keeping her hands in plain view. "Um, I think there's been a mistake," Mary said.

"She said that a missing person was dead but no one else would know it," the officer reported. "She admitted that she killed him."

"I did not," Mary argued.

"You asked me if I believed in ghosts," he said. "That means you killed him."

"No, that means I saw his ghost," Mary replied.

"Ma'am?" one of the officers asked. "Did you really say you saw his ghost?"

"Mary, think before you speak," Mike cautioned, looking back and forth between Mary and the two police officers with guns.

Exhaling slowly, Mary met the officer's eyes. "Yes, officer, I did say that," she replied. "And, unfortunately, he could not remember his last name."

"That's not really what I meant," Mike exclaimed. "These guys have guns, Mary."

The door opened again, and this time a woman dressed in a white polo shirt and navy blue slacks with a gold badge on her belt walked in. She quickly glanced around the room and then took a good look at Mary. "Aren't you Chief Alden's wife, from Freeport?" she asked.

"Oh, good, the cavalry," Mike said.

Mary nodded. "Guilty as charged, Chief Chase."

"And didn't you used to be a Chicago police officer?" she continued.

"Yes, I was," Mary answered.

"So would you mind explaining to me what's going on here?" she asked and then turned to her officers. "I think you can put away your weapons, officers. I can personally vouch for Mrs. Alden."

"Finally, someone with a little sense," Mike said, and then he studied the chief's face. "Wait, I think I know her."

The officers quickly holstered their weapons and stood at ease. Then the chief turned back to Mary. "You were going to explain."

"I believe your desk officer got the wrong impression from an answer I gave him when he was doing a missing persons search for me," she said. "He thought I had killed the subject."

"And why would he think that?" she asked.

84

"Because when he asked me if the subject was deceased, I told him that he was but his records wouldn't show it."

"And how did you come by that information?" she asked.

Mary sighed softly. "I saw his ghost," she said.

Mike groaned loudly. "Really, Mary?" he said. "Did you not remember that answer has not really worked twice today?"

Chief Chase studied Mary for a moment without saying a word. Finally, she nodded. "Why don't you join me in my office, Mrs. Alden," she suggested. "And we can discuss this in private."

"Could I get the search results before we leave?" Mary asked.

Chief Chase shook her head. "No, we'll leave those here for now," she said.

Mary followed the chief down a narrow hall to her office. The room was not as large as Bradley's office, and the equipment not nearly as new. But Mary realized Galena had a fraction of the population of Freeport.

"Please, have a chair," Chief Chase offered, pointing to a very uncomfortable-looking metal chair with rust-colored plastic cushions on the other side of her desk.

Mary complied immediately, folding her hands on her lap and patiently waiting for the first question.

"So you believe you can see ghosts?" the chief asked.

Mary shook her head slightly and saw the look of relief of the chief's face. "No, I don't just *believe* I can see ghosts," Mary replied. "I *can* see ghosts."

"Yeah, good job, Mary," Mike said, slipping through the wall and standing next to Mary. "Always stay with a winning strategy."

Chief Chase sat back in her chair and studied Mary's calm face. "That's an unusual response," she finally said.

Mary smiled. "Yes, it is," she said. "And I know what most people think when they find out about my…unique ability. And believe me, there have been many times in my life when I would much rather not have this particular gift, but that's the way it goes."

"I've got it," Mike said. "I do know her. I dated her."

Surprised, Mary turned to Mike. "You dated her?" she asked, and then, recalling where she was, she covered her mouth with her hands.

"I'm sorry?" the chief asked. "Who were you just speaking with?"

"Um, this might sound strange, but do remember Mike Richards?" she asked. "He was a fireman in Freeport."

"Yes, I remember Mike," she said, the pleasant look on her face darkening. "We dated a few times, and then he never returned my call."

Mary turned to Mike, a look of astonishment on her face. "Really?" she asked.

She turned back to the woman across the desk from her. "Actually, you might not have heard," she said. "But Mike died a couple of years ago."

The chief stood up. "Mike's dead?" she exclaimed. "No, I didn't know."

Mary nodded. "It actually turned out that he was murdered," she said. "Poisoned."

"So that's why he never called me?" she asked.

"Yeah, not really," Mike replied. "But we can sure tell her that to make her feel better."

"Mike is here, right now," Mary said. "And he told me that I can tell you that his death was the reason he didn't call you."

"Way to lie without lying, Mary," Mike said, clapping his hands.

"How do I know you're telling the truth?" Chief Chase asked.

"Her first name is Chelsea. She likes old movies, and she has a tiny heart tattoo on her left cheek," he said with a fond smile.

Mary looked at the woman across from her. "She doesn't have a tattoo on her cheek,"

Chelsea turned bright red, and Mike chuckled. "Her other cheeks, Mary," he explained.

"Oh," Mary said, biting her lower lip in embarrassment and looking at Chelsea. "I'm sorry. That was embarrassing."

"How did you know about my…," she paused for a moment and cleared her throat. "My tattoo?"

"Mike told me," she replied. "He told me that your first name is Chelsea, although I could have remembered that from the first time we met. I didn't, sorry, but that really doesn't prove anything. He said you like old movies, and he told me about your tattoo."

"Ask him where he took me for our first date," she said, crossing her arms over her chest and raising her eyebrow in challenge.

"So, Mike, where did you take her?" Mary asked.

"I hate those kinds of questions, Mary," he complained. "Why do all women think that men can remember stuff like that?"

"Think, Mike, it's important," Mary urged him.

"*What color dress did I wear when you first saw me?*" Mike asked in falsetto. "*How did I do my hair?* No one gives a guy credit for remembering a girl's name."

"Mike, you don't get points for remembering a woman's name," Mary lectured. "A woman wants to think she was memorable, not just another flash in the pan. I can't believe you don't remember your first date with her."

Chelsea's mouth dropped open, and she stared at Mary. "It would be just like him to forget where we went."

"Well, I remember that we had ribs together and you let me lick the sauce off your—"

"Mike, too much information," Mary called, and then she turned to Chelsea. "He does remember you ate ribs together, and it got messy."

Chelsea nodded and sighed softly. "Good old Mike."

"Yeah, good old Mike," Mary agreed. "So, Chelsea, how about those search results?"

Chapter Nineteen

A ringing sound from her purse stopped Mary mid-stride as she walked back down Main Street in Galena. Stepping to the side, she glanced down to the small pocket on the outside of her purse, specifically designed to hold her phone. Of course it was empty. "Crap," she muttered, opening her filled purse to begin the frantic search. Guided by the ringing and the vibration, she was finally able to find it beneath her billfold. Quickly swiping her finger across the front to answer the call, she held the phone to her ear.

"Hello?"

"You forgot to put your phone back in its little pocket, didn't you?" Bradley asked, a smile in his voice.

Sighing, she nodded. "Yeah, I was in a hurry, so I just dumped it into my purse."

"And you've already found it," he replied. "I'm impressed."

"Bradley," she said.

"Yes, Mary?"

"Shut up," she said, grinning into the phone.

"Before I shut up can I tell you I got an address in Dubuque?" he asked.

"You got an address for Liza's parents?" she exclaimed. "That's fantastic. What is it?"

Mary waited a moment for Bradley to respond. "Bradley?" she urged.

"So here's the deal," he finally said. "I'm taking the afternoon off, and I'll meet you in Galena. Then we will drive together to Dubuque and meet with this family."

"But—" she began.

"No buts," he interrupted. "We have no idea who these people are and what part they played in Liza's death. It's just too dangerous for you to go there alone."

He took a deep breath and waited for her argument.

She thought about it, thought about arguing that she was a professional and could handle things. She thought about how many times as a Chicago police officer she'd knocked on doors far more dangerous than this one potentially was. She thought about the fact that she would have to wait for forty-five minutes before he could even reach Galena. And then she thought about the pain and worry she'd seen in his eyes that morning. He wasn't questioning her abilities. He just needed to protect her.

"Bradley," she finally said.

"Yes, Mary."

"I'll call Katie and let her know we'll be picking up Clarissa a little late today," she said.

She heard him release the breath he'd been holding. "Great," he replied. "I'll leave right away."

"And Bradley," she added.

"Yes?"

"Thank you for coming with me."

There was a slight pause on his end. "Thank you for understanding why I needed to do it."

She hung up the phone with a smile in her heart and placed it, carefully, back in the outside pocket of her purse.

"So, we've got forty-five minutes to kill," Mary said to Mike. "Pardon the pun. What should we do?"

Mike glanced up the street. "Well, Amelia's been waving at you for the past five minutes," he replied. "Maybe she'll have a suggestion."

Hurrying down the street, Mary met her friend in front of her shop. "Hi, what's up?" Mary asked.

Holding one hand behind her back, Amelia pulled a keychain from her pocket with her other hand and held it out to Mary. "Donna stopped by and left this for you. It's an extra key," she said. "She said if you were in town and wanted to stop by her apartment to see if Liza was there, that would be fine with her."

"Perfect," Mary said, taking the key. "I can go over there now. What great luck. And here my horoscope told me my luck was going to be bad this week."

"Well," Amelia said with a slight frown and pulling her other hand out from behind her back. "This is for you, too. I found it on your car."

Mary looked down at the small piece of paper in Amelia's hand. "A ticket?" she exclaimed. "I got a parking ticket? Well, crap. I never get parking tickets."

Mike cleared his throat pointedly.

"Okay, I almost never get parking tickets," she amended.

He cleared this throat one more time.

"Okay," she sighed, glancing at Mike. "I hardly ever get parking tickets outside of Freeport."

Amelia giggled. "Do you have your very own invisible conscience with you?"

Glancing at Mike again, Mary grinned. "Yeah, give someone the title of guardian angel, and you can't get away with much," she teased. "Of course, he is handy to have around when you get arrested."

"You got arrested?" Amelia gasped.

Shrugging, Mary nodded. "Well, not officially. Mostly I got questioned."

"About?" Amelia asked.

"I just happened to mention that I knew someone was dead but no one else knew," she explained.

"Well, I can see why that might raise a few eyebrows," Amelia replied, biting back a smile. "So, how did you get off?"

"I had a little inside information about the chief from my guardian angel," she said. "So, once she realized he was in the room with us, it wasn't a far leap for her to realize the dead guy spoke to me, too."

"Really?" Amelia asked, clearly not convinced.

"Okay," Mary sighed, rolling her eyes. "The fact that I was married to Bradley probably helped more. Professional courtesy and all that."

"So, the ticket's for ten bucks," Amelia teased, waving the paper under Mary's nose. "You gonna fight it?"

Mary snatched the ticket from Amelia and stuffed it in her purse. "No, I'll pay it and consider it a deal," she said.

Amelia laughed. "Maybe you can write it off as a business expense," she teased.

"You're not helping," Mary said.

Amelia shrugged. "Hey, it was your horoscope, not mine," she said.

Chapter Twenty

"I like Amelia," Mike said, seated in the passenger seat as they drove up Main Street to Donna's apartment. "She's got a great sense of humor."

"Says the guy who didn't get the ticket," Mary grumbled good-naturedly.

"Says the person who didn't get murdered," Mike countered.

Mary glanced over at him, relieved that he was grinning. "Okay, you win," Mary admitted, pulling up in front of Donna's apartment. She looked up to the third floor windows, hoping to see the little girl's face there.

"I can't see her," Mike said, peering in the same direction.

"I don't see her either," Mary said. "But I wouldn't be surprised if she stayed away from windows because she is afraid."

He looked at her. "Ready to walk up three flights of stairs?" he asked.

She nodded. "Ready."

A few minutes later they were entering the small apartment. Mary closed the door behind her and turned towards the small living room where Liza had been the last time she'd seen her. The room was empty. "Liza," Mary called softly. "Liza, its Mary. Can you come out and speak with me?"

A soft light appeared in the corner of the living room. It grew larger until it was the size of the little girl, and finally, she came into focus a few feet away.

"Hi, Liza," Mary said with a smile. "I want you to meet a friend of mine. His name is Mike."

The child looked up at the angel and studied him. "I saw you last time," she said. "You're not like the other ones."

Mike squatted down so he was closer to her height. "No, sweetheart," he said. "I'm more like you. I'm an angel."

She studied him for a few more minutes. "Are angels from God?" she asked.

He smiled and nodded. "Yes, angels are from God."

Her face darkened, and she shook her head. "I don't like you."

"Why not?" Mary asked, surprised.

Liza turned to Mary and pointed at Mike. "He's bad. He hates little girls. He hurts little girls."

Mike shook his head. "No, sweetheart, I don't hate little girls," he said, keeping his voice calm even though his heart was breaking for her. "I protect little girls."

"No, you're from God, just like the bad man," she said. "He was from God, too, and he hurt little girls."

"The bad man?" Mary asked. "The one who adopted you?"

Liza nodded. "He told the second mommy he was from God," she said. "And then he took me and hurt me."

"He wasn't from God," Mike said. "He might have said it, but he really wasn't from God."

She put her hands over her ears. "You're wrong," she screamed at Mike. "You're wrong. He was from God. God took away my mommy and daddy. God took away my next mommy and daddy.

God gave me to the bad man. And the bad man from God hurt me. I hate God."

"Sweetheart," Mike said, moving closer to her.

"No!" she screamed. "Stay away from me."

"Mike," Mary said.

"Yeah, I know," Mike said, moving back and disappearing through the door.

Liza watched him go, and then she slipped her hands from her ears. "Where did he go?" she asked.

"He knew he was upsetting you," Mary explained. "So he went outside so you wouldn't be afraid anymore."

She paused for a moment and stared at the door. Then she turned her little swollen eyes to Mary. "Is he a bad man, too?" she asked.

Mary sat down on the edge of the coffee table so she could be a little closer to the child. "No, Mike is not a bad man," she said. "He is a good man. He saved a little girl who was about your age when a bad man was coming to get her."

"He saved her?" she asked.

Mary nodded. "Yes, he did," she replied. "He's an angel and he protected her."

A tiny, translucent tear slipped down the pale cheek and glittered brightly as the little girl slowly faded away. Her voice was sad and quivered as she asked her final question before she disappeared. "Why didn't God send an angel to save me?"

Chapter Twenty-one

Mary opened the door and found Mike on the other side, leaning against the wall. He was staring off into space, and the sorrow on his face broke Mary's heart. "She's gone," she said softly. "Why don't you come back inside?"

Pushing himself away from the wall, he nodded once and floated in front of her into the apartment. He didn't meet her eyes but instead moved away from her to look out the window. "She was really afraid of me," he said softly. "Not just afraid, but terrified. I've never seen a child so frightened."

Mary closed the door softly and leaned against it. "It wasn't you, Mike. She wasn't afraid of you; she was terrified of memories of what happened to her, how she was murdered," Mary said. "But I don't understand what she meant about him being from God."

Still staring out the window, Mike shrugged. "Maybe he was one of those religious zealots who justify abuse by twisting the words of God," he said. "Maybe he quoted scripture to her as he abused her."

She watched him, his back straight and his voice laced with anger. She knew that if he was still a human he would be punching the wall to release some of the anger and frustration. "We'll find out, Mike," she said. "We'll find out who he is and what he did, and he'll be punished."

He sighed and leaned forward, his head against the window frame. "I heard her," he said, his voice a mere whisper. "And I don't know how to answer her question."

"Which question?" Mary asked.

He turned, and the bleakness in his eyes almost frightened her. "Why didn't God send an angel to save her?" he asked, his voice thick with emotion. "Why, Mary? Do you know the answer to that?"

She shook her head. "No, I don't," she said, walking over to him. "I often ask myself that question, too. Why did a beautiful little girl die of cancer? Why did the young soldier get killed in an explosion? Why did the young mother die in a car accident? What about all of those innocent victims who are shot every day in the streets of our country? Why didn't God step in and save them all?"

"And what do you do when you ask those questions and don't have an answer?" he asked.

She paused for a moment to think about her answer. She met his eyes and then looked away, through the window at the street below. "I can only remember a little bit about when I died," she said softly. "I remember that all the pain stopped. I remember this intense feeling of peace and well-being. I moved forward, toward this bright light that didn't hurt my eyes. It felt warm and welcoming, like coming back home after a long trip."

She turned to him. "Then I was given a choice," she said. "I really wanted to continue. I really wanted to go there to the light. But, for a quick instant, I saw my family in the waiting room. I saw my father's face, drawn and pale. I saw my mother weeping in his arms. I saw Sean, his jaw clenched and his hands clamped together to control his emotions. And I knew, no matter what I wanted, I needed to go back."

"What does this have to do with Liza's question?" he asked, moving away from the window and walking across the room. "You were an adult. You had a choice. You got to go back home."

"Mike, when I was coming back to earth, to my family," Mary explained gently, tears forming in her eyes, "I realized that it wasn't home. Home was behind me. And even though it broke my heart to come back, I knew someday I'd return."

She took a deep breath and wiped her eyes. "When I ask myself that question, how could God let those people die? I remember that he didn't let them die. He just brought them home."

He just stared at her for a moment, silent tears slipping down his cheeks. "You're right. I'd forgotten how I felt. I was so concerned about getting back down here to help you, asking for permission to be a guardian angel, that I really didn't think about my surroundings," he said quietly. "But I remember it felt like home when I finally crossed over."

"I always wondered how you found the strength to leave," she said. "I never even made it all the way to the light, and I didn't want to return. But you were there."

"I think it's different for an angel," he replied thoughtfully. "We're still linked to the light, even though we're here. I didn't have to give up as much as you did."

"I'm glad you're here, Mike," she said. "You are the angel that God sent to help Liza."

He looked surprised, and then a small smile formed on his lips. "We need to find this guy so Liza can finally go home," he said.

"Yes, we do," she agreed, smiling back at him. "And we will."

Chapter Twenty-two

Standing on the sidewalk in front of Donna's apartment, Mary gazed down Main Street for Bradley's cruiser and then pulled out her phone to check the time. There was still about five minutes before he was scheduled to be there, but Mary was anxious to meet the people who had given Liza away.

Taking a deep breath, she slightly chastised herself, "Just take it easy. He'll be here in a few minutes."

She made a point of stepping back mentally and studying her surroundings. The afternoon sun was still hot, and Mary could see heat waves rising from the sidewalk at the end of the street. The sounds of Main Street were like a summer orchestra; the cicadas' song was an underlying buzz of bass beneath the higher sounds of traffic, conversation, and canned music from the storefronts. The scents of Main Street were again eclectic and mouthwatering; a mix of specialty shop aromas, from chocolate to popcorn, mixed with the scent of freshly ground coffee from the gourmet bean shops. Those combined with the tangy smells of meat grilling from the steak houses and garlic and oregano from the Italian restaurants.

She felt a wave of serenity wash over her as she closed her eyes and breathed in deeply once more.

"You're smelling the chocolate, aren't you?" Mike asked.

"Shhhhh," she whispered. "I'm having a food fantasy."

He chuckled. "I don't want to disturb your daydream," he said, "but Bradley just parked the car down the street."

She opened her eyes immediately and looked down the street. Bradley, dressed in his khaki police uniform, stepped out of the car and glanced down the street, assessing the area quickly. When he caught Mary's eyes, he smiled, and her heart quickened.

He walked towards her with an easy, athletic stride that accentuated his long legs and broad shoulders. Mary sighed appreciatively. "He is such a hunk," she said.

"Yeah, if you go for that kind of obvious, all-American, incredibly masculine, hero type of guy," Mike replied.

Mary sighed again. "Yeah, if you go for that type," she repeated with a wide smile.

"It seems that you're not the only one who appreciates that type," Mike commented, noting the interest of more than a few female tourists who stopped window shopping to gaze at him appreciatively. A few more aggressive ones smiled invitingly in his direction when he passed by.

"He doesn't even see them," Mike said.

"Yeah, I noticed," Mary replied, a wide grin on her face as Bradley reached them.

"Hi," she said, reaching up to kiss him.

He looped his arms around her waist and held her lightly. "Hi yourself," he replied, gazing into her eyes. "I missed you."

He tightened his hold and bent over, softly tasting the edges of her lips, teasing her, until he was driving her crazy. She softly moaned, slid her hands up through his hair and held him in place so her lips could be firmly fixed on his. His seductive chuckle of appreciation sent a wave of passion through her body, and she shivered in his arms. He deepened the kiss, giving them both more of what they wanted but not enough to satiate the burning in her abdomen.

"Um, I hate to interrupt your reunion, but you are standing on a public street. And, you do have an appointment in Dubuque," Mike reminded them. "And while you two are out of town, it's my job to keep an eye on Clarissa, so I've got to get out of here."

Bradley straightened up, Mary still in his arms, and exhaled slowly as he looked down at his wife. "Did I happen to mention that you look incredibly sexy today?" he asked.

Shaking her head, she smiled up at him. "Yeah, I've heard that a protruding belly is fairly hot," she replied ironically, "especially for the Santa Claus crowd."

He stepped back and placed his hands on her belly. "A tiny belly with our baby in it is extremely hot," he replied, his face sincere. "Never forget that."

"I won't," she said. "So, not that I minded, but why did you walk up here? I thought we were going in your car?"

He shrugged and tried to hide the glint in his eyes. "Well, I thought that the cruiser was less likely to get a parking ticket in Galena."

"How did you know?" she asked, astonished. "How could you possibly know?"

She turned to Mike. "Did you tell him?"

"Don't look at me," Mike said, holding his hands up defensively. "I've been with you the whole time."

She turned back to Bradley. "Bradley, listen—" she began.

"The department called me once they ran the plates and discovered whose car it was," he interrupted with a smile. "They called to apologize. They said they had detained you, so it was entirely their fault you were late in moving your car."

She breathed a sigh of relief. "Well, I'm glad they admitted they were at fault."

He nodded. "I also had a very interesting conversation with Chelsea Chase," he continued. "She apologized for interrogating and nearly arresting my wife."

Mary bit her lower lip. "Well, that was nice of her," she muttered.

"And when were you going to tell me that you had been held at gunpoint at a police station?" he asked.

Her heart dropped a little. She was really hoping she could have kept that incident a secret. "Quite honestly, I was sort of hoping it would never come up in the conversation," she replied.

"Mary, I worry—"

She lifted her hand and placed it over his mouth. "You don't need to worry," she said. "If I hadn't been able to handle it, you would have been the first person I called. I promise."

He kissed her hand, and she dropped it. "Promise?" he asked.

"Promise," she replied.

Mike winked at her. "Sure you would," he whispered.

"Shhhh," Mary replied over her shoulder. "You're going to get me in trouble."

Bradley looked back and forth between Mary and Mike. "What are you two up to now?" he asked.

Mike shook his head. "Nothing, Chief," he said with a smile. "I'm just heading back to Freeport. Have a great time in Dubuque."

As Mike faded away, Bradley offered his arm to Mary. "Let's take the cruiser," he suggested. "I think you've freaked out the whole Galena Police Department enough that you are never going to get a ticket here again."

"Bonus!" she replied.

Chapter Twenty-three

The ride to Dubuque only took about twenty minutes from Galena. Once they were on the four-lane bridge over the Mississippi River, Mary had a clear view of the prosperous river town. A huge three-story steamboat was moored off the bank of the river in the distance. And like its predecessors that used to roam the great river a hundred years ago, it housed a casino. Another smaller steamboat was anchored farther west in a small inlet amidst a collection of red-bricked buildings and industrial docks waiting for the next barge to be unloaded and sent back on its way.

From the river, the city rose onto a bluff, and from her vantage point on the bridge, Mary could see the 190-foot tower of the Dubuque County Courthouse with its fourteen-foot-tall, bronzed Lady Justice at its pinnacle. The downtown, with its collection of historic and modern buildings, lay at its feet, and the grand, residential palaces of yesteryear dotted the hillside with their varied and unique architecture.

Once across the river, Bradley stayed on Highway 20 through the city until he reached its far western borders. He turned right on JFK Boulevard into an area that quickly changed from a collection of malls to one of residential neighborhoods. It took only ten minutes to reach the small, brick bungalow on Kimberly Avenue whose address matched their information. Bradley drove past the house and parked farther down the street.

"So, how do you want to handle this?" Mary asked.

"I think if we present it as an official investigation we'll probably get more cooperation," Bradley said. "So, how about if I take lead?"

"I agree," she said. "I'll introduce myself as an investigator working on the case."

They left the car and walked up the street to the house. The backyard was visible from the front sidewalk, and Mary could see that it was littered with toys and playground equipment.

"They have children," she said. "I wonder if they are younger or older than Liza."

Soon after they knocked on the door, a pleasant looking woman answered the door. Her smile froze when she saw Bradley's uniform.

"Mrs. Larson?" Bradley asked. "Mrs. Lorraine Larson?"

"Is everything okay?" she asked abruptly, her voice filled with fear.

"Yes, ma'am," Bradley replied professionally, offering her his identification. "I'm Police Chief Bradley Alden from the Freeport Police Department. We are here about an investigation regarding a child who used to live in this household."

Mary was surprised by Bradley's cold demeanor, but she took his lead. "May we come in and ask you a few questions?" she asked.

The woman stepped back and opened her door wider. "Yes, of course," she stammered.

"Is your husband home?" Bradley asked.

"Yes, he is," she said. "Please have a seat. I'll go get him."

Bradley and Mary entered a small living room with worn but comfortable furniture. There was a white brick fireplace with a mantle in the middle of one wall. On the top of the mantle was a collection of family photos. Most of the photos featured a smiling set of twin boys with their parents, but one photo, obviously taken years ago, added a dainty little girl to the family. Bradley picked up the photo and showed it to Mary. "Was this Liza?" he asked.

Mary nodded. "She's a little older now," she said quietly, "but, yes, that's her."

His jaw tightened, and he put the photo back in place.

"They must still have feelings for her," Mary suggested, "or they wouldn't have a picture of her on their mantle."

He shook his head. "We'll see," he said.

He turned sharply when he heard footsteps in the hall. Lorraine and her husband hurried into the room.

"This is my husband, Mark," Lorraine said. "Mark, this is Chief Alden and…"

Mary stepped forward and offered her hand to Mark. "I'm Mary O'Reilly, a private investigator working on this case with Chief Alden."

"Good to meet you," Mark said cordially. "How can we help you?"

"Are your children home?" Bradley asked.

"Yes, they're down in the playroom," Lorraine replied.

Bradley nodded. "We won't take too much of your time," he said. "Is there a place where we can talk so your children will not overhear our conversation?"

Lorraine nodded slowly. "Yes," she said. "Come into the dining room."

Once seated around the table, Bradley pulled out the report he had received from the county. "We are looking into the whereabouts of Liza Parker," he said. "We understand you adopted her in 2009."

Lorraine reached over, took hold of her husband's hand and took a deep breath. "We…we don't have her anymore," she said.

"I'm sorry," Bradley said. "You don't have her anymore? But you did legally adopt her, didn't you?"

Mark nodded. "Yes, of course we did," he said. "But she's not with us any longer."

"Did she pass away when she was in your care?" he asked. "Because the county has no record of a death certificate."

"Oh, no, nothing like that," Lorraine said. "I got sick. Cancer. Just after we adopted her. The doctor said that I needed to simplify my life, so we found another family who wanted to adopt Liza."

"And what governmental or legal agencies did you work with in order to proceed with that adoption?" Bradley asked.

Mark cleared his throat. "Well, actually, we needed to move quicker than that, so we went with another avenue."

"Another avenue?" Bradley asked, his voice clipped.

"Well, yes," Lorraine said. "A friend told us about an adoption website where you could re-home an adopted child."

"Re-home?" Bradley asked. "And exactly how do you do that?"

"You place an ad about your child on this forum, and families looking for children contact you," Lorraine said. "Then you meet with them, and they sign a paper consenting to be her legal guardian."

"And that's all?" Bradley asked. "Did you do a background check on these people?"

"Of course," Mark said. "We paid for a background check, and it came out just fine. We wouldn't just give Liza away to anyone."

"Do you still have a copy of that background check?" he asked.

Lorraine nodded. "Yes, I have it in my file cabinet," she said. "We wanted to keep it so some time in the future we could possibly go and visit her again."

"Could you please get that for me?" Bradley asked.

Lorraine stood and hurried out of the room.

"How is your wife doing now?" Mary asked.

Mark smiled. "Her cancer is in remission," he said. "She's been fine for about a year and a half now."

"That's wonderful," Mary said. "So Liza was given up for adoption how many years ago?"

"About three years ago," Mark said. "When we first learned about the cancer."

"And your other children," Bradley asked. "Your twin boys, what did you do with them?"

Surprised, Mark shook his head. "Well, we kept them, of course," he said. "They are our children."

"And Liza wasn't your child?" Bradley asked.

"Well, yes," Mark began. "But, you know, we had just adopted her. She wasn't attached to us yet. We thought it was in her best interest…"

His voice trailed off when Lorraine came into the room.

"I made a copy of the papers," she said eagerly. "You can keep this copy."

Bradley reached over and took the papers from her, scanning them quickly. He looked up and met her eyes. "Thank you for your help," he said, standing up and moving towards the door.

Mary quickly stood and followed him.

"Is Liza okay?" Lorraine asked, rushing after him to the door. "Is she missing?"

Bradley stopped, slowly turned around and faced the parents.

"Bradley," Mary warned. "Don't."

"Liza is dead," Bradley said, ignoring Mary's request. "She was brutally murdered."

Lorraine collapsed against her husband. "No," she sobbed, her voice rising to a cry. "No, that can't be true."

Chapter Twenty-four

Bradley turned and opened the door, letting Mary outside before he followed her. He pulled the door closed behind him, muffling the sobs of despair.

"Bradley?" Mary asked, turning to him.

"Give me a minute, Mary," he said. "Then we can talk."

They walked down the street together in silence. Bradley opened the door for Mary, helped her in and then entered on the other side. Mary sat quietly, watching his internal struggle, and waited for him to begin the conversation. She'd seen this kind of reaction before when she was a cop in Chicago. Sometimes when a crime was so horrific or hit too close to home, an officer needed a few minutes to process it. They needed to get past the anger and the rage, to tamp down the frustration, and be able to professionally get their minds around the crime without letting emotion compromise their judgment. Mary had experienced the feeling more than once, especially in cases of child abuse. She needed to step back and remember that she wasn't the judge and jury. She was an officer of the law, and she had to work within its guidelines.

They drove back down Highway 20, but just before the bridge, Bradley turned to the left and drove through the side streets to a small park on the bank of the Mississippi. He pulled into the parking lot, put the cruiser in park, and turned to Mary. "I need to tell you something before I answer your questions," he said.

"Sure, whatever you need," she said.

He turned and looked out the windshield watching the river flowing past them. "The reason I knew about re-homing wasn't because of new laws against it," he said, "although Wisconsin is working on laws to make it illegal. It was because of the increase of child trafficking on the Mississippi."

"What?" Mary asked. "Child trafficking here in the Midwest?"

He nodded. "The Mississippi offers access to two different borders, a number of major highways and a number of large cities. Beyond that, there have been an increased number of websites that feature child pornography or live-streaming sexual child abuse throughout the Midwest."

Bradley leaned forward, placing his head on the steering wheel for a moment, and then he turned back to her. "Mary, some of these kids who are being sold for sex are as young as three years old," he said. "There is no limit to the sickness that is out in the world today. The streaming websites don't only show child sexual abuse, but in many cases they also show the child being violently abused."

He pounded his fist against the steering wheel. "And people pay money to watch it," he said, his voice thick with anger. "There are sick people, really sick and unbalanced people out there, and these people, the Larsons, gave a little girl away like you would give a puppy away."

"How bad is it?" Mary asked.

"It's estimated that there are between 100,000 and 300,000 children in the United States at risk for commercial sexual exploitation and one million children exploited by the global commercial sex trade each year. The average age of these kids is twelve. Twelve years old, Mary. And Liza was only five."

"Is that why you were so harsh with the Larsons?" she asked. "To be fair, we don't know that's what happened to Liza. She could have just been abused by someone. We can't know she was trafficked."

He sat back in the chair, closed his eyes and shook his head. "Your description of what happened to Liza reminded me of a victim's report I read," he confessed. "I made a couple of calls and discovered that another young girl was found floating in the Mississippi with marks similar to those on Liza. I also discovered that soon after her death, a porn video showing the young victim being abused was shown from an IP address coming from outside the United States."

Mary felt sick to her stomach. "Was anyone arrested?" she asked. "Do they know who did it?"

He sat up and met her eyes. "The agency looking into this believes that it started as a streaming event," he said.

"What? People watched it real time? They saw a little girl being abused, and they didn't report it?"

"They not only didn't report it, they paid to watch it," he explained. "It was streamed live and recorded and then sold from an international distributor. Mary, people make a lot of money catering to the depraved people out there."

"So, whoever we're looking for," she said, "whoever killed Liza, could potentially be running some kind of pornography operation?"

"Yes, and as the money increases, so does the danger," he said pointedly.

She saw the look in his eyes, and she was having none of it. "Oh, no. Don't tell me you want me to give up on this case," she said.

He studied her for a moment and then shook his head. "No, I won't do that," he agreed. "But I want to work with you on this one. I want to be in on everything. Agreed?"

"Yes, of course," she said, and then she placed her hands on her abdomen. "What kind of world are we bringing our baby into?" she asked quietly.

She felt his hand cover hers, felt the warmth and reassurance. "Hopefully a better one," he said.

Chapter Twenty-five

"So how was your day?" Clarissa asked Mary as they set the table for dinner.

"It was very interesting," Mary said, trying to inject some normalcy into an otherwise crazy day. "How was your day?"

"It was great," Clarissa said. "Mrs. Brennan told us about Friday the 13th and how it can be lucky or unlucky."

"Really?" Bradley asked from the kitchen where he browned hamburger in a cast iron pan. "I thought it could only be unlucky."

Shaking her head, Clarissa placed a napkin next to a plate. "One thing you can do is wear red underpants," she said with a giggle.

A knife slipped from Mary's hand and dropped to the floor. "Red underpants?" Mary asked, bending over and picking it up. "Are you teasing me?"

"No, I promise," she laughed. "Red underpants are good luck, so you should wear them on Friday the 13th."

"I guess I'll have to go out tomorrow and get us all red underpants," Mary said, putting the knife in the sink and getting a fresh one from the drawer.

"Are there any other things we can do?" Bradley asked. "I'm not really a red underwear kind of guy."

Clarissa thought for a moment. "Oh, yeah, you have to get out of bed on the right side of the bed," she said.

"Which side is the right side?" Bradley asked.

"The side that's not the left side," Mary replied.

"Oh, that kind of right side," Bradley said. "Well, that's my side anyway. So I don't know if it will be luckier."

"Well, you're not supposed to clean your house on Friday the 13th," Clarissa added, "because holding a broom is bad luck and so is doing laundry."

"We're having the party here on Friday afternoon," Mary said. "Do you think using a vacuum cleaner is okay?"

"I guess," Clarissa said. "She didn't say anything about that."

"Well, we don't believe in superstitions anyway," Bradley said.

Reaching across the counter, Bradley's sleeve caught on the salt shaker and it fell over, spilling salt on the table. He righted the shaker and automatically picked some of the spilled salt up and threw it over his left shoulder.

"Why did you do that?" Clarissa asked.

"What?" Bradley asked.

"Why did throw salt over your shoulder?"

Mary grinned at him. "Yes, Mr. We-Don't-Believe-In-Superstitions-Anyway, why did you throw salt over your shoulder after you spilled it?"

Shrugging, Bradley sent an embarrassed smile to both of the ladies in his life. "Well, we don't believe in all superstitions," he amended.

Mary winked at Clarissa. "So, what size would you like those red underpants to be in?" she called to Bradley.

"Funny, Mary, very funny," he replied.

Clarissa climbed into her chair and Mary sat next to her. "Do you think it's bad luck to have the baby's party on Friday the 13th?" she asked.

Mary leaned over, hugged her and placed a kiss on her forehead. "No, I think by bringing everyone we love together to celebrate the new baby we will have greater power than bad luck, and we will turn Friday the 13th into a lucky day," she said. "Besides, Rosie will be making the food for us, so how can it be unlucky?"

Nodding, Clarissa leaned towards Mary and lowered her voice. "Yeah, but Daddy will be grilling, and he burns stuff," she said.

"I heard that," Bradley called, walking over to the edge of the counter. "And I don't always burn things. Sometimes I serve them raw."

"And sometimes they're burnt on the outside and raw on the inside," Clarissa added.

"Well, that takes a pretty talented cook to do that," Mary said, winking at her daughter. "Wouldn't you agree?"

Giggling, Clarissa nodded. "Yes, really talented," she agreed. "Is that what Stanley means when he says it should be a crime what Daddy does to a steak?"

"Yes," Mary replied quickly, grinning at Bradley. "That's exactly what it means. The meat is so good, it's a crime."

"Stanley sure is funny," Clarissa said.

"Yeah, he sure is," Bradley muttered. "As funny as a broken bone."

"Um, Bradley," Mary said, trying not to laugh.

"Yes?" he asked.

"I think the hamburger is burning," she said, biting back a smile.

Bradley turned to see smoke rising from the cast iron frying pan. He hurried over to the stove, picked up the pan and carried it to the sink. He turned on the cold water faucet, and they all heard a loud hiss as a puff of steam encased both Bradley and the sink.

A moment later, Bradley walked around the counter and sat at the table with them. Sighing, he pulled out his phone and turned to Mary and Clarissa. "So, do you want pizza or Chinese?" he asked.

Chapter Twenty-six

Gigi Amoretti walked back to the ancient outbuildings behind their home. She had the option of taking an underground passageway between the house and the outbuilding, but the idea of walking down the dark, narrow tunnel always made her squeamish. Instead, she preferred the star-studded, evening sky and the cool, evening breezes carrying the scent of field corn.

Like a silent behemoth appearing in the darkness of the night sky, the barn stood with faded paint, broken windows and rotted planks of barn wood that indicated a building that had stood in disrepair for too long to be salvaged. She lifted up the metal latch that held the Dutch door closed and then looked over her shoulder before pulling the door open and slipping inside the dark barn.

But that darkness lasted for only a moment until Gigi reached over and pressed the high-tech touchscreen panel embedded in the wall. Suddenly, a large array of fluorescent bulbs flickered to life, flooding the area with light. Brightly enameled walls, looking nothing like the inside of an old barn, reflected the light onto a gray concrete floor. A crisscrossed pattern of scaffolding suspended several feet below the twenty-foot-high ceiling held movable wall partitions, green screens, backdrops, high powered lighting and remote controlled cameras. Thick black cables snaked from the equipment across the ceiling. It looked like a Hollywood soundstage complete with a small editing and control booth in the corner.

Her high heels echoed loudly as she crossed from the door all the way across the building to the door of the control booth. She flipped on the light switch to the room and made her way to the control bank in front of the large, picture window. Sitting on the leather chair, she pressed a button that illuminated the control panel, including a small computer.

She looked up to her left where a television screen displayed closed circuit security camera views for the front of the house, the road, and the front of the barn. Noting that no one was nearby, she flipped another switch. A loud, mechanical rumble nearly shook the building as a portion of the roof opened, and a satellite dish on a hydraulic stand raised up to above the top of the barn and the tree line. Once the dish was in place, Gigi checked the connection speed and smiled. "Perfect," she murmured.

Flipping another switch on the panel, a large screen ascended from beneath a hidden panel in the next room. The screen copied the view of her computer monitor. Adjusting the switch labeled "Camera One," she maneuvered the camera until the same screen showed up on the camera feed on another monitor in the control room. She watched until the clock was at 7:59, and then she began to type.

DUE TO CIRCUMSTANCES BEYOND OUR CONTROL, TONIGHT'S WEBSTREAM IS CANCELED. AS PER YOUR BUYER'S AGREEMENT, YOU WILL NOT BE RECEIVING A REFUND; HOWEVER, YOU WILL RECEIVE VIEWING RIGHTS TO OUR NEXT PRESENTATION. THANK YOU FOR YOUR UNDERSTANDING.

She watched the words from the keyboard appear on the monitor, the screen, and finally the camera. Almost immediately the phone in front of her rang and she picked it up without hesitation.

"Yes?" she asked casually, tapping her fingers on the aluminum panel. "I understand you're disappointed. No more than we. But sometimes things happen that we cannot control."

She waited while the caller spoke, her eyes narrowing and her lips thinning. "May I remind you that I have maintained a client list of all transactions made with this company?" she stated. "And should that list ever fall into the hands of the authorities in your country, I dare say that even you, in your lofty position, would face certain consequences. People are so funny about having their elected officials partake in sadomasochistic voyeurism, especially when children are involved."

She smiled triumphantly and nodded. "Yes, of course I understand that you were merely overwrought," she soothed. "And because you are one of our very best clients, I will be happy to send you a free DVD of the next event so you can relive the thrill at your leisure."

She listened for a moment longer, yawning quietly as he spoke. "Of course, we are searching for a replacement as we speak," she promised, "someone even better than previously advertised."

She nodded again. "À bientôt," she said, hanging up the phone.

She sat back in the chair, tapping her fingers on the panel, and waited to see if she would be receiving any more negative feedback. One thing she had learned, you had to keep the customers happy and coming back for more. Sometimes it required a reminder of their vulnerability, but usually it just required a production that satisfied all of their peculiar cravings.

As she waited, she opened another screen on the computer, accessed the re-homing forum and started to read down the lists. She quickly discarded any posts about infants; they were too much trouble and no use to her. Although some of her clients' tastes did run to children that young, they could go elsewhere for that kind of entertainment.

Finally, she found one that interested her and reread it with growing delight.

Ursula is ten years old. She is a beautiful girl from Portugal, and we adopted her six months ago. She has only been able to learn a few words of English in the time she has been with us. We believe she may be mentally slow and will need special help, which we cannot afford. If you are interested in meeting Ursula and speaking with us about re-homing, please private message us.

With a satisfied smile, Gigi logged into the forum under her username "pastorswife" and started to type her response.

You are an answer to our prayers…

Chapter Twenty-seven

Mary poured the hot water from her coffee maker into her oversized mug. The tea bag lying in the cup danced and swirled as it met with the hot water. She sighed softly. She knew she shouldn't have eaten those last couple pieces of pizza, but they looked so good. And today she was paying the price. She hoped the chamomile and ginger in the tea would help calm her stomach. She picked up the tea, sniffed the fragrant steam rising from it and smiled. Relief was only a few minutes away.

She walked to her desk, put the cup on top of the coaster and started to sit down when she felt a swift kick to her abdomen. But the kick was from the inside out. She froze, her eyes wide with wonder. She slowly slid her hand to her belly and waited.

Thump.

There it was again. Her baby. She just felt her baby kick.

Tear-filled eyes looked up when the door of her office opened.

"Mary," Bradley began, and then he stopped, realizing she was bent over her desk, clenching her stomach with tears in her eyes. "What's wrong?"

He rushed to her side and placed his arm around her, trying to guide her to the chair. "Is it the baby?" he asked.

She nodded happily, tears sliding down her cheeks. "I felt the baby," she whispered in awe. "The baby kicked me."

He slid his hand over hers. "Here?" he asked. "You felt the kick here?"

She looked up at him and nodded again. "We are having a martial arts expert," she said, her voice brimming with laughter. "You should have felt the power of that kick."

They both fell silent, waiting to feel the baby again.

"There!" Mary cried. "Did you feel it?"

Bradley shook his head. "No, I didn't," he said.

She pulled her hand out from under his and guided his hand to the spot. "Now, you're closer," she said, holding his hand tightly against her body. "Wait for it."

Breathing slowed, all their concentration focused on their hands, they waited.

Thump.

"There!" she cried happily. "Did you feel it?"

Bradley seemed less impressed. "Kind of," he said. "It was like you hiccupped."

"No, it was a major kick," she argued. "Didn't you feel it?"

He shook his head. "Not really," he admitted.

She sighed. "Well, maybe because the kick came from inside me, I can feel it more," she reasoned.

"Makes sense," he agreed. "But I'm sure in a couple of weeks I'll be able to feel them, too."

She put her hands on her belly, feeling another little kick. "So, I kind of get a sneak preview of coming attractions," she said.

Bradley leaned over and kissed her forehead. "Seems only fair since you have to do all the hard work."

She sighed and cuddled into him. "Bradley," she whispered.

"What?" he whispered back.

123

She reached up on her toes so her mouth was next to his ear. "We're going to have a baby."

He wrapped his arms around her and hugged her. "Yes, I know."

"But now it feels so real," she explained. "I mean, I feel our baby. This is actually going to happen."

He smiled down at her. "Yeah, this is actually going to happen," he said. "And I can't wait."

Chapter Twenty-eight

Joey Amoretti stumbled out of his bedroom and made his way down the hall, following the scent of coffee. He blindly reached for a mug and poured himself a cup of the dark brown liquid. Nearly scalding his tongue, he gulped down half a cup before he turned to his wife, who was sitting at the kitchen table reading the morning paper, already dressed and ready for the day.

"You didn't come to bed last night," he grumbled.

"I had things to do," Gigi replied, her eyes not leaving the newsprint. "We have an appointment this afternoon down in Quincy."

"Quincy?" he scowled. "That's more than three damn hours away. I drove all day yesterday. I ain't driving again today."

She slowly lowered the paper and looked at him, her stare angry and cold. "I beg your pardon?"

Scuttling back, he sloshed hot coffee on his hands. Juggling the mug back to the counter, he dropped it with a crash and then grabbed a dishtowel to blot up the remaining coffee. "I'm sorry, my dear," he apologized. "I didn't mean any disrespect. I wasn't thinking straight."

She continued to stare at him like a panther toying with its prey. He twisted the dishtowel nervously in his hands. "Sweetheart?" he ventured.

"You do recall what I do to people who cross me," she said casually, although her tone didn't fool him.

He swallowed and shook his head. "Yes, I do," he replied.

"You do recall how I took care of the threat to our enterprise, don't you?" she asked.

He immediately pictured the four large gravesites in the woods beyond the barn, nestled between smaller ones and remembered the looks of surprised bewilderment on the faces of the builders when Gigi nonchalantly shot them each in the forehead. She had anxiously waited for them to appear the morning after she had reviewed the nighttime security footage revealing that one of them had returned, unannounced, to the barn. "Yes, dear, I do," he replied.

"Then don't make a nuisance of yourself," she said, picking up her cup of tea and sipping delicately.

Brushing the perspiration off his forehead, he nodded at her. "I'll just go wash up," he said. "Won't take me but a moment. Then we can be on our way."

"Wear your light blue suit," she ordered, picking up the paper again and scanning the columns. "And make sure you shave."

Joey was dressed and ready to go in record time. He had recovered his good mood by drinking enough whiskey to dull the pain, but not enough for Gigi to detect. "You gonna tell me about the merchandise?" he asked.

"I'll tell you all about her as we drive down," she replied. "And this time you'd better control yourself. We have very angry subscribers who are looking for an event worth the money they've spent."

"We taking her home with us tonight?" he asked as they drove south towards Quincy, Illinois.

Gigi shook her head. "No, we are only meeting with the parents to demonstrate what loving and caring Christians we are," she replied scornfully. "And once we convince them how saintly we are and, of course, give them the right information for a background check, we will be picking up our newest daughter within the week."

Joey chuckled maliciously. "It's like taking candy from a baby," he said. "It's so easy when you are dealing with people who aren't as smart as you are."

Gigi glanced over at Joey, derision in her eyes, and just shook her head. "Yes. It is."

Chapter Twenty-nine

Mary studied the missing persons reports she received from the Galena Police Department looking for Steve. Out of the half dozen reports she had received, she had narrowed it down to a possibility of two different men. Sighing, she glanced at the phone on her desk, willing it to ring. Bradley was running a background check on the family who had taken Liza, and he promised he'd call as soon as the results came in.

"Why are you staring at your phone?"

Startled, Mary looked over to see Steve sitting on the other side of her desk.

"Good morning," she said.

"Really? Good morning?" he asked caustically. "The last time we met you dropped the bombshell that I'm dead, and all you can say to me is good morning?"

She started to apologize then shook her head. I am not going to be bullied by a ghost, she thought angrily.

"Listen, Steve," she said, leaning forward aggressively on her desk, then catching a whiff of him and changing her mind. "I didn't kill you. I didn't have anything to do with your death. I'm taking time out of my life to help figure out what happened to you, to help find you. And if you think you can just appear before me smelling like a crap and having an attitude that's worse than your smell, well, then you can just crawl back into your mine shaft and wait for the next guy to rescue you."

Abashed, Steve sighed and slowly nodded his head. "You're right," he said. "You're trying to help me, and I've been a jerk."

Mary gave a little. "Well, I understand that finding out you are dead can be a little bit of a shock," she said.

His lips turned up in a small curve. "Well, yeah, that can pretty much ruin your plans for the rest of your day," he said, "or your life."

Chuckling softly, she nodded. "Yeah, I can see that."

She pulled out two reports and slid them across the desk. "I've been going through the missing persons reports from the Galena Police Department," she explained. "And these two reports seem to fit you best. A friend of mine, Andy, who lives in Galena, suggested you might have fallen into an old mine shaft on your property and were never discovered."

Steve thought about it for a moment. "I remember there was light, and then, suddenly, there was darkness and pain," he said. "As I was falling, I hit against the rock wall a couple of times, hitting my head, my shoulder, my leg. And when I finally landed, it was in what seemed to be a river or quicksand. But it was too dark. I couldn't see."

Taking a shaky breath, he closed his eyes for a moment and then looked at Mary.

"The water closed over my head," he said. "I couldn't breathe; I thought I was going to drown. I was flailing my arms around, trying to grab hold of something, anything to pull myself up."

Looking down, he held his hands out in front of himself. "Finally, I grabbed onto the rock wall. It was limestone and slippery, but I could dig my fingers in and pull myself up, out of the water."

He stopped and closed his eyes once again, trying to remember. "My leg," he said, opening his eyes as the memories returned. "My leg wouldn't move. It must have been broken. I bobbed down in the water, trying to touch the bottom, but it was deeper than six feet, so I kept clinging to the wall. I screamed for help, over and over, until my throat was raw and I couldn't scream any longer."

Pausing for a moment, he looked up at the ceiling, tears forming in his eyes. "I was so alone," he said. "But I didn't want to die."

He took another deep breath and continued. "I was exhausted, but I knew if I fell asleep I would lose my hold on the rock and I'd drown," he said. "So I dug my fingers into the rock, looking for little crevices for support. I climbed up, dragging my leg behind me. The first time, I got about two feet up, and I lost my grip and slipped down the rock wall. I scraped my face, and my body and was plunged back into the water. But, I pulled myself back up and I tried again."

He looked at Mary. "I had to live," he said. "I had to get back to my kids."

Mary nodded. "Yes, I understand," she said.

"I started the process again," he continued, "slowly pulling myself up using my hands and arms. It was dark, so I really didn't know where I was going; I just felt my way along. Finally, I think I was about four feet above the water, and I found a cave. I think it was a cave. Anyway, there was enough room for me to climb in and rest. I was cold and shivering, but more than that, I was exhausted. So, I lay down against the rock and went to sleep."

"You did everything you could to get back to your family," she said. "My friend Andy said the mine shaft might have been covered with sod, so no one knew what had happened to you."

"I don't want my kids to think I left them," he said. "I don't want them to think I didn't love them enough to stick around."

Nodding, Mary pulled the reports back across the desk and scanned them. "Okay, does the name Steve Sonn sound familiar?"

His eyes widened, and he slowly nodded. "Yes, Steve Sonn," he said, his voice growing with excitement. "That's me. That's who I am. I'm Steve Sonn. Mary, you're a genius."

"Well, it was a fifty-fifty chance," she replied. "So, not a lot of genius was required."

"Well, what do we do next?" he asked. "When can I see my kids?"

"According to the report, you've been missing for about twenty years," Mary explained. "So, your kids will be close to the age you were when you died."

"I've missed their whole lives," he said sadly. "I missed everything. Baseball games, Christmases, birthdays, graduations. I wasn't there for them."

"That wasn't your choice," Mary reminded him. "You would have been there if you could."

"They don't know that," he said. "All they know is their dad left them."

"Okay," Mary said, pulling her keyboard in front of her and typing. "Then we'll let them know the truth."

Steve leaned forward. "How? How are you going to find them twenty years later?"

"I'm going to do a web search for them," she said. "They probably have some kind of social media listing."

"A web search? Social media? What are you talking about?" he asked.

Mary looked up from her computer screen. "Wow, that's right. Twenty years has really made a difference in the world hasn't it?"

The results came back for his oldest son's name, and Mary clicked on a popular social networking site. "Why don't I show you rather than try to explain it," she said, turning her computer monitor so Steve could view it, too.

A page with photos of Steve's son, Gregg, and his family showed on the screen. "That's Greggie," Steve said, pointing to the little boy in the photo who looked to be about six years old. "He hasn't changed at all."

Mary shook her head. "No," she said, pointing to the man holding the child. "That's Greggie, and that's his son, Stevie."

Steve looked up, tears filling his eyes. "He named his son Stevie?" he asked.

Mary nodded. "Yes, he did."

"Thank you, Mary," he said with a tearful smile. "Now all we have to do is find me."

Mary nodded. "Yes," she said. "And I'll start working on that right away."

He started to fade away. "Stevie," he whispered. "I have a grandson named Stevie."

Chapter Thirty

Mary knocked on the door of Bradley's office and then peeked in. Bradley, his phone to his ear, smiled at her and motioned her forward. She softly closed the door behind her and sat in the chair on the other side of his desk.

"Yes, Chris, we're pursuing some leads here," Bradley said into the phone. "I'm willing to share whatever we discover, and if you could do the same that would be great."

He paused for a moment to listen. "Okay, fine," he replied. "And thanks for the information. I really appreciate it. Goodbye."

He hung up the phone and turned to Mary. "That was Chris Thorne. He was in my unit in the service. He's FBI now and has been working with the state's Cyber Crime Division. I called him yesterday to tell him that we were following up on what could be a child trafficking situation, and he just called to tell me that one of the IP addresses they've been tracking for the web streams carried a different kind of data last night. It connected with a re-homing forum, and the user name "pastorswife" was affiliated with it. The user connected with someone looking to re-home a little girl. But the rest of the conversation was through private messages, so they couldn't get more information."

"Why don't they just get a geographical link to the IP address?" she asked.

"Whoever is operating this porn site has got some technical abilities," he said. "They're using a proxy server, most likely a VPN or virtual private network, which encrypts their data and hides their identity. So, they don't even know if the IP address is good. For all they know, "pastorswife" could be a well-meaning woman trying to help."

Mary sighed in frustration. "Well, at least we have a lead on Liza," she said.

"Well, yeah, about that," Bradley said. "I did a background check on the family we got from the Larsons. They live up in Madison, and their record is clean except for a couple of parking tickets. But it doesn't seem like they had Liza for very long. All of their kids are registered to a local school, but there was never a registration for someone Liza's age."

"So, we don't need to drive up to Madison?" Mary asked.

Bradley shook his head. "No, I think a phone call will do it," he replied picking up the phone. "I'll put it on speaker, but I think it would be better if you handled the interview, especially if the mom answers."

She nodded and pulled out a notepad and a pen.

Bradley tapped in the numbers and set the phone to speaker.

Within a few rings it was answered.

"Hello?" a woman's voice responded on the other line.

"Hi, my name is Mary O'Reilly. May I speak with Melody Greyland?"

"This is Melody."

"Hi, Melody. I'm a private investigator and I'm trying to locate Liza Parker," she said.

"Oh, wow, have you been hired by her parents?" she asked. "Do they want her back?"

"Well, because of client confidentiality, I can't really say," Mary said apologetically. "But I can tell you it's something like that."

"That's so cool," Melody said. "I think kids should be with their natural parents. And Liza was such a cute kid."

"So, you knew Liza?"

"Oh, sure. Yeah. She lived with us for a couple of weeks, but it didn't really work out," she said. "So, we were able to find another family to take her. No big deal."

Mary saw the anger and frustration cross Bradley's face.

"Do you happen to have the contact information for that family?" Mary asked, keeping her voice friendly and light.

"Sure do," she said. "Bruce, my husband, said we needed to keep it with our important papers in case something went wrong and we needed to prove that they accepted guardianship. He was real worried that if she got sick or something, someone would come after us for payment."

"Well, that was really smart of him," Mary said.

"Yeah, he's always thinking of stuff like that," she agreed. "He wanted to be a lawyer. I actually have it scanned on our computer. Do you just want me to email you a copy?"

"That would be great," Mary said, offering her email address.

"I'll send it to you right away," Melody said. "Do you need anything else?"

"Do you remember anything about the family she went to?" Mary asked. "It might make things easier when I talk to them."

135

"Oh, yeah, they were great," she said. "He was a pastor, really into helping kids and teaching them about God. They had just come back from a trip to some country where they helped run an orphanage. They missed the children so much they decided to adopt some children of their own. Isn't that great?"

"Yes, that sure is great," Mary repeated. "You don't happen to remember their user name, do you?"

Melody laughed. "How could I forget it?" she asked. "It was "pastorswife." Cute, huh?"

"Yeah, real cute," Mary said. "Thanks again, Melody."

"Hey, no problem," she said. "Oh, if you see Liza, tell her Melody says hi."

Mary nodded. "I will," she said. "Goodbye."

Bradley pressed a button and disconnected the phone. For a few moments neither of them said a word, just stared at the phone in the middle of the table. "She didn't even give Liza a second thought," Mary finally said. "It just didn't work out. I can't believe someone would say that."

"I have a feeling background checks on the good pastor and his wife aren't going to turn up anything," Bradley said. "But at least we can report back that the user name "pastorswife" has been used before in a re-homing situation."

"We can say more than that," Mary said. "We can tell them they murdered Liza."

Bradley shook his head. "Not unless we have a body and proof they did it," Bradley said. "A body just tells us that she was buried in an unmarked grave. Anyone could have buried her. They could have buried her after she died of a disease. No one has reported her missing. There is no investigation. We have to be very careful with this one, Mary. We need to be sure we have solid proof."

Chapter Thirty-one

Bradley hung up his phone, sat back in his chair and ran a hand through his hair.

"It's not good news, is it?" Mary asked.

For the past hour, Bradley had been on the phone with his friend Chris and various other law enforcement agencies along the Illinois, Iowa and Wisconsin borders to see if they had any information that would help bring them closer to the location of the phony minister and wife.

He shook his head. "So far it's a dead end," he said. "Most people who give children away really don't like to get the police involved. And it looks like this couple is smart, so they've covered their tracks."

The phone rang before Mary could respond, and Bradley picked it up.

"Chief Alden," he said and then waited while the caller identified himself. "Thanks for calling back. I'm working on a case, potential child trafficking, and I've got a couple of persons of interest who are posing as a minister and his wife. The MO seems to be that they pick up adopted kids whom the parents want to re-home and then traffic them. I'm looking for anything that might lead us to their location."

He paused a moment, and his eyes widened with interest. "What? You're kidding," he said, excitement growing in his voice. "This is great. Yeah, if you could get me their information, I'll give them a call. It sure sounds like a match. And if you wouldn't mind forwarding their descriptions on to the FBI, I think they'd be interested, too."

Grabbing a notepad and a pen, he quickly jotted down some information. "Hey, thanks a lot," he replied. "Yeah, you have a good one, too."

"What?" Mary asked as soon as he hung up the phone.

"It was the Clinton Police Department," he said. "A guy called yesterday and said he and his wife met with a couple at a restaurant at the edge of town. They had been thinking about re-homing their adopted daughter but changed their mind. He said the minister got pretty irate and didn't act like a minister, in his opinion. He said both of them creeped him out and seemed to look guilty, so he called."

"Oh, wow, that's great," Mary said. "That's got to be our guys."

Bradley picked up the phone and dialed. "There's only one way to find out."

A few minutes later Bradley hung up his phone and sat back in his chair. "They got nothing," he said. "No license plate, no identification, no address, no phone number. These creeps really know how to cover their tracks."

Mike appeared in the office and looked from Mary to Bradley. "Hey, what's wrong?" he asked.

"We thought we had a lead on the people who killed Liza," Mary explained, "but it was a dead end."

"So, what do we know?" Mike asked.

"We know there's a couple out there, posing as a minister and his wife who are adopting children," Bradley said. "And they are active along the Mississippi River area."

"We know that this couple adopted Liza and killed her," Mary added. "That was the man of God who hurt her."

138

"We know they are still trying to adopt children in the area," Bradley added. "They had a failed attempt yesterday, and it looks like they were on the Internet last night trying to find another child."

"We have a good description of the two of them that's been forwarded to the FBI," Bradley said. "And I'm sure they'll be running them through their database, but these two are smart. I don't think they'll find anything."

Mary shook her head. "So what do we do now?"

"Well, if it were me," Mike said, "I'd ask Liza."

"Ask Liza what?" Bradley asked.

"Where they buried her," he said. "Or where she lived."

Mary shook her head. "She was only five, she wouldn't…"

She stopped and stared at Mike for a moment. "You're brilliant," she said. "Liza won't remember, but Donna and Ryan will remember where they first met Liza. It can't be too far from where she was buried. She wouldn't have wandered that far on her own."

Bradley nodded. "Yeah, she only came with Ryan when he asked Donna if Liza could come home with them," he agreed. "That's got to be our starting place."

"Let's just hope Ryan and Donna weren't in Florida when it happened," Mike said.

Mary pulled out her cell phone. "Well, there's only one way to find out."

Chapter Thirty-two

Bradley drove the cruiser through the town of Galena, past the downtown area and to the other side of town where he turned left on a small rural road that led almost directly west. They drove past farms and fields with corn stalks reaching over six feet high. Further down the road, the farms were interspersed with small woods as the road curved around a sharp bend.

"Okay, Donna said her dad's farm was just at the end of this bend," Mary said, "on the right-hand side."

Slowing the cruiser, Bradley found the nearly hidden driveway and pulled up the long lane to the farmhouse. Before he could turn off the car, a man in his late fifties walked out the front door and watched them from the top step of the wide, wraparound porch.

Bradley got out of the car first and walked around the car, putting himself between the man and Mary. "Hi," Bradley called, lifting his hand to shade it from the bright, midday sun. "Are you Donna's dad?"

The man nodded and slowly came down the steps. "Yep, I am," he said slowly. "You that psychic person from Freeport?"

Biting back a smile, Bradley shook his head. "No, that would be my lovely wife," he said. "I'm the Chief of Police in Freeport."

He shook his head. "So that's why there's a police car in my driveway," he said. "I wondered about that."

Mary slipped out of the car and joined Bradley. "Hello, Mr. McIntyre," she said. "I'm Mary. I've met your daughter Donna and your grandson Ryan."

Nodding, he studied her. "So Donna tells me," he said. "She said you're helping her out."

"Yes, I hope to help her," Mary said, "and the little girl Ryan met."

"I seem to remember him mentioning her to me," he said hesitantly. "How much are you charging her to do this?"

Knowing he was only trying to protect his family, Mary took a deep breath and pushed the anger away. "I'm not charging them anything," she said. "I'm not a fraud or a con-woman; I just investigate things like this."

Yeah, that's what Donna said, too," he replied, coming forward to shake her hand. "I just needed to make sure myself. So, what can I do to help?"

"Donna thought that Ryan met Liza here, when he was visiting," Mary explained. "All we want to do is investigate the areas of your property where Ryan might have played."

He brought his hand to his hips and gazed out over his property. "Well, he and I have purt near covered every inch of my 150 acres. But, as I recall, the day he found his invisible friend we were out near the river fishing."

"Where's the river from here?" Bradley asked.

Mr. McIntyre pointed through the woods. "It's down that path about a mile or so," he said. "You can use the ATV to get down there, and then you'll have to walk the river path. We were up and down that river all day."

141

Mary looked down the narrow path that seemed to disappear into the thick woods. "We just follow that path until we get to the river?" she asked.

A half-smile grew on the man's face. "Yes, ma'am," he said. "And if you get wet, you've gone a bit too far."

Bradley chuckled. "We appreciate the loan of your ATV," he said, "and we'll bring it back to you in good shape."

"If you want, I can hook up the boat trailer to it," the man offered. "Not much of a boat, just a rowboat, but it's better than wading."

"We'd appreciate it," Bradley said. "You never know where something like this will lead."

Chapter Thirty-three

"Where the in the world is this path leading?" Mary asked. She brushed another corn stalk out of her face as they rode down the narrow path.

"It's going to the river," Bradley shouted over the roar of the ATV's engine. The high-end, four-seater vehicle had superior suspension and drove over the bumpy cornfield like a dream.

Bradley slowly maneuvered the vehicle to the other side of the road to avoid hitting a small bump in the road.

Mary looked down at the speedometer from her vantage point in the passenger's seat. "Bradley, you're only going five miles an hour," she exclaimed. "This baby can fly through this field. Open her up."

He turned to her. "I'm not risking you or the baby for some crazy ride in a cornfield," he said.

"Bradley, it was bumpier riding in the cruiser on the gravel road on the way up here," she said. "I'll be fine."

"Mary, we're not in a race here," he said.

"But we want to be back before dark," she replied, and then she looked around. "Do you know where we are?"

He paused for a moment before answering. "Yes," he finally said. "It's a short cut. I know where I'm going."

She shook her head. "Oh, no, that's man code for you are totally lost," she said. "We should turn around and get directions."

Bradley shook his head. "Well, we haven't hit water yet, so I think we're on the right path."

"I think you took a wrong turn at the V in the road," Mary said, looking over her shoulder, "when you were watching out for bumps. We are driving in the middle of a corn field. Mr. McIntyre didn't say anything about a corn field."

"His whole farm is a cornfield," Bradley argued, inadvertently pressing on the gas pedal as he turned to Mary. "Of course he didn't say anything about it. That would be redundant."

"You still should let me drive," she said. "I have more experience."

"You grew up in Chicago," he responded. "How could you have more experience?"

"I never got lost in the forest preserves," she replied. "I never got lost on the lakefront. I never got lost—"

"Mary, I'm not lost," Bradley interrupted. "I know exactly where I—"

"Bradley! Stop!" she screamed as they suddenly burst from the cornfield and onto the narrow bank of the river.

Bradley turned the ATV sharply, sending a spray of muddy river water onto Mary. Her face splattered with drops of mud, she turned to Bradley, streams of water flowing down her face. "You knew exactly where you were going?" she asked. "So you planned this?"

Pulling a handkerchief from his pocket, he gently wiped the mud from around her eyes. She could see that he was having a hard time containing his laughter. "Would you believe I knew where I was going, but I just got there faster than I planned?" he asked her.

"No," she replied decisively. "I would not believe that."

He leaned forward and kissed her dirty forehead. "Would you believe I'm sorry?"

Lifting her hands to the sides of his face, she held him in place as she leaned forward and rubbed her cheek against his, sharing her dirt with him. She leaned back and smiled. "Okay, now I believe you're sorry," she said.

He reached up and felt the mud. "Thanks for sharing," he replied.

She grinned. "Anytime."

"Hey, are you okay over there?" a man's voice called from the other side of the river.

Oh, great, Mary thought, *of course someone would be here to see me covered in mud.*

"We're fine," Mary called back.

"Who are you talking to?" Bradley asked.

Eyes widening, she looked at Bradley and then slowly turned and looked across the river. A man dressed in blue jeans and a muddy work shirt stood on the opposite bank. He was about six feet tall, had brown hair and a bullet hole in the middle of his forehead. Mary grabbed Bradley's arm with one hand and pointed to the man across the river with the other.

"What the hell?" Bradley asked when he saw him.

They climbed off the ATV and walked to the edge of the bank. "Hi," Mary called. "Can we help you?"

The man shook his head. "No, it's too late to help me," he said. "I don't want to alarm you or anything, but I'm dead."

Chapter Thirty-four

Mary nodded. "Yes, we actually noticed that," she said. "How did it happen?"

"I got shot," the man shouted back.

"Yes, I noticed that, too," Mary replied, and then she turned to Bradley. "This is Police Chief Alden. Do you want to report a crime?"

"You're a cop?" the man yelled at Bradley.

"Yes, I'm a cop," Bradley called back.

"Well, I've got some information for you," he said. "Can you come over to this side of the river? I hate shouting because someone might hear us."

Bradley glanced at Mary, and they shared a sad smile. "Actually," Mary said, "it might be easier for you to come over to us. Just think about crossing the river."

The man stared at Mary, his hands on his hips, and shook his head. "I've never been a water guy," he said. "I don't think—"

Suddenly he disappeared and then just as quickly reappeared a few feet from the ATV. "Hey!" he cried, surprised. Then he gazed around. "Well, cool."

Disembarking from the ATV, Mary and Bradley walked over to him.

"Hi, I'm Mary," she said. "And, as I mentioned earlier, this is Bradley."

He held out his hand to shake, but unfortunately, it glided through Mary's hand. He jumped back. "Whoa," he said. "That's creepy."

Mary nodded. "Yeah, it takes a little getting used to. So, who are you?"

"Oh, sorry, I'm Bill, Bill Patterson," he said. "I own…well, I used to own Patterson Construction in Dubuque."

"Hi. Bill," she replied. "If you don't mind me asking, how did you die?"

"I got shot," he said.

"Yes, that's what I thought," Mary replied. "But perhaps you could fill us in on the details."

"Oh, yeah, right, the details," Bill said. "Okay, well, we took this job over the river."

"Over the river?" Bradley asked.

"Yeah, it was in Illinois, I'm a licensed contractor in Iowa, so, really, I'm not supposed to be working over the river," Bill explained.

"Okay, got it," Bradley said. "So you took this job, and it was under the table."

"Yeah, it was a cash job," he said. "No contracts, no invoices, nothing. Strictly do the work and get the cash. I even told the office we were going fishing in Wisconsin. I figured it was like Christmas money for the four of us."

"There were four of you?" Mary asked. "Are the other guys okay?"

He shook his head and sighed. "No, they got shot, too," he said, his voice dropping to a whisper. "And I'm to blame. I got my buddies killed."

"How?" Bradley asked.

He took another deep breath. "So, I'm redoing this barn for a minister and his wife," he began.

"Excuse me," Bradley interrupted. "Did you say a minister and his wife?"

"Yeah, but they didn't look like church people to me, and they didn't sound like church people when they spoke to each other," he said. "I should have listened to my gut. My gut is never wrong."

147

"What did your gut tell you?" Mary asked.

"That these two were up to no good," he replied. "I mean why does a minister need a state-of-the-art sound stage with satellite hookups and everything out in the middle of nowhere?"

"What did they tell you?" Bradley asked.

"They told me they were going to broadcast their sermons worldwide and bring the good news to third world countries," he said. "Sounded good at first, but then I got to thinking. What kind of third world countries got Internet hookups to watch sermons in the first place? Know what I mean?"

"So, what happened to you?" Mary encouraged. "Why do you think you got your friends killed?"

"So, we left for the night, and I'm nearly to the bridge when I realize I left my cell phone back at the work site," he said. "I drive back and don't want to bother nobody, so I turn off my truck lights when I get to the driveway and quietly drive back to the barn. I go inside and find my phone just where I left it, next to the table saw. So I pick it up and turn to leave when I notice there's a light coming from the other side of the room, the control room. I quietly sneak over there and I see the minister and his wife reviewing a film they've made. I figure it might be interesting to peek at the film, I mean the minister's wife was not a bad looking woman."."

He paused and looked back over the river. "What I saw," he said, shaking his head in disgust. "What I saw the minister do to that little Hispanic girl. It was revolting. It was beyond revolting. I should have called the police. I should have reported him right then and there."

"But you didn't?" Bradley asked.

148

"I figured it was too late for the kid," he admitted. "I could tell she was dead by the time the film was finished. So, I figured we'd all come the next day, get our gear, and then call the cops. You know, don't leave any evidence that we were there."

Mary nodded. "Because it was an over the river deal."

"Yeah," he said. "Exactly. I thought I was pretty quiet when I drove out of there. I drove about a mile, then pulled over and barfed my guts up. I called the guys and told them that we were going to pull out the next day, but I didn't tell them why."

"How did they find out?" Bradley asked.

"Hell if I know," Bill replied. "We show up the next morning, acting like nothing's wrong, and the little lady comes out. She's carrying a basket like she's bringing us a treat, but it's got a gun inside. She pulls it out, and she's smiling. And we're backing away, screaming at her. But she doesn't even flinch. Bang, bang, bang, bang. Like shooting fish in a barrel, me and the guys are dead."

"And you never got to talk to the police," Mary said, realizing the reason Bill hadn't crossed over.

"Yeah, I never got a chance," he said. "And I've been watching them. They've been doing more of that stuff. They got a bunch of graves back in the woods. They went out again today, and I think they're trying to get another kid."

"Well Bill, you've just reported it to the police," Bradley said. "And I have a friend in the FBI who has been looking for these two. Thanks, Bill. You may have saved a little girl's life."

"You guys want me to show you the house and the barn?" he asked. "There are all kinds of secret panels and stuff like that inside."

149

Mary started to agree, but Bradley caught her arm and shook his head. "As much as we'd like to head over there and investigate, unless we get a search warrant and do this the right way, these two could get off on a technicality," he said. "And I'm not willing to risk that."

Mary sighed. Bradley was right. "I have to agree," Mary said. "But they don't have any children there right now, do they?"

Bill shook his head. "Naw, they went for a first meeting today," he said. "If they follow their pattern, they'll either bring the girl back tonight or go back and get her tomorrow afternoon. It don't seem to take too long for whatever process they use."

"I'll call my friend, and we'll get back here as soon as we can," Bradley promised.

"You don't mind if I stick around, do you?" Bill asked. "I could maybe help you in the raid."

Bradley, instinctively barring a civilian from being in on a raid, started to shake his head.

"Bradley," Mary whispered, interrupting him. "Remember, Bill's dead."

Pausing mid-comment, Bradley shook his head slightly. "One of these days I'm going to get used to this," he said and then he turned to Bill. "Yes, I would really appreciate your expertise on the raid."

"Okay, I'll be watching for you," Bill said, slowly fading away. "Thanks, Chief."

Chapter Thirty-five

"Chris, this is Bradley," Bradley said into his cell phone as he stood next to his cruiser in Mr. McIntyre's driveway. "I have a…a trustworthy source that has identified the minister and his wife and the soundstage they use for web streaming."

Mary sat in a chair on the front porch watching his expression as he spoke.

"Here you go, young lady," Mr. McIntyre said, handing Mary a damp hand cloth. "That'll take some of those mud freckles off your face."

Smiling up at him, Mary wiped away the remaining traces of mud and handed it back to him. "Good as new," she said.

He looked her over and shook his head. "Well, if you're planning on going anywhere but home, I'd suggest you put a jacket over your blouse."

Looking down, Mary saw that the "mud freckles" extended all the way down the front of her shirt. "That's the last time I let him drive," she muttered.

Mr. McIntyre chuckled. "There's just something about men and ATVs," he said. "Turns 'em all into boys again."

He looked over at Bradley. "So, did you find what you were looking for?" he asked.

Mary nodded. "And then some," she replied. "And your help has been invaluable. Thanks for letting us search your property."

Bradley tucked his phone into his pocket, and Mary took that as a signal to stand up. "Thanks again," she repeated.

"No problem," the older man said. "You just call if you need any other help."

Mary walked over to the cruiser while Bradley waved goodbye to Mr. McIntyre, and a moment later they were driving down his narrow driveway back to the road.

"So?" Mary asked.

"Chris is going to pull together a group using local law enforcement and some of the guys from the Chicago office," he said. "He'd like to hit the house early in the morning before they leave."

"Okay, so where do we meet him?" she asked.

He paused and just looked at her for a moment.

"No," she said before he could comment. "You are not going to ask me to stay home. I realize the danger; I've been on raids before. I'll wear Kevlar if it will make you happy. But I am the only one who can communicate with Bill, and that could give us vital information to catch them."

Sighing, he nodded and looked forward, tightening his jaw. "I don't like it," he said.

"Yeah, I know," she replied. "But you mostly don't like it because I'm right."

He nodded slowly. "Yeah, exactly."

"Sorry," she said. "You can ask Chris to keep us together on the raid if that will make you feel better."

"Yeah, it will," he said. "And I already did."

"Good. I was hoping you would," she said, sliding her hand over to lay on his. "I want to lock these two up and throw away the key."

"Yeah, if there was ever a crime that warranted the death penalty, this would be it," Bradley said. "But since Illinois is a no death penalty state, I hope they put them somewhere dark and deep and never let them see the light of day."

Mary sat up straighter in her seat. "Oh, that reminds me," she said, quickly pulling out her phone and checking the time. "It's still early afternoon, would you mind if we stopped in Galena?"

"Sure, no problem," Bradley said as he turned onto Highway 20. "Where would you like to go?"

She smiled over at him. "My favorite place to spend an afternoon," she said. "The police department of course."

Chapter Thirty-six

Bradley and Mary stood in front of the building that housed the Galena Police Department. "Are you really sure you want to go in there?" Bradley asked.

Mary nodded. "Yes. As difficult as this might be, I really need to get the search for Steve started."

"Well, I'm right here to back you up," he said, placing his hand on the small of her back and guiding her into the building. "So, if they think you're crazy, they'll have to think I'm crazy, too."

She grinned at him. "That's so reassuring, darling," she said.

They opened the door to the reception area, and the same officer that had panicked the last time Mary was in sat behind the desk. "Hi again," Mary said. "I'm here to see Chief Chase."

The young officer looked beyond Mary to Bradley. "Have you taken her under custody, sir?" he asked.

Bradley stared down the young man with the same look he used on young recruits in the service. "Actually, officer, this is my wife," he said. "And I'm here to help her resolve an issue regarding one of the citizens of your town."

The young man swallowed hard and nodded. "I apologize, sir, ma'am," he said. "I'll call the chief right away."

A few minutes later they were both sitting on the other side of Chief Chase's desk. "Chief Alden, Mrs. Alden, what can I do to help you?" she asked, sitting back in her chair and studying them.

Mary smiled inwardly, recognizing the posture as a typical interrogation position. So, Chief Chase still wasn't sure about her abilities. Well, that was understandable; it had taken a decapitated ghost and a haunting in her own home to convince Bradley.

She leaned forward and smiled, another interrogation pose. Two could play this game.

"If I were sitting in your chair, I would think the people sitting across from me were nuts," Mary said. "So, I appreciate you taking some time out of your day to visit with us."

Chief Chase merely nodded but didn't change her position. "Well, I consider it a professional courtesy," she replied.

Ouch, Mary thought. Well, let's see how far that courtesy goes.

"Well, whether you believe me or not," Mary said, "I can see and communicate with ghosts. It began after a near-death experience when I was shot in the line of duty as a Chicago police officer. I've had psychological screenings and I can give you the personal phone number of the doctor who met with me. Her official report states that she does not feel that I have any psychological or physiological effects from the shooting, but because of my new ability, I would be distracted while on the job."

She sat back in her chair. "So, we can take the time for you to call Dr. Gracie Williams and have her convince you, or you can, for a few minutes, have a willing suspension of disbelief and listen to what I'm going to say with an open mind."

Mary waited, watching the chief for any signs of agreement. Finally, with a loud sigh, Chief Chase sat forward, her elbows on her desk and nodded. "Okay, convince me."

"Earlier in the week I was in Galena on another case," Mary began. "And I saw a movement out of the corner of my eye. I ended up on High Street speaking with the ghost of Steven Sonn. All he could tell me at the time was his first name and that he was in a dark place."

"Like hell?" Chief Chase asked, not bothering to hide her sarcasm.

Mary glanced up at the clock in the Chief's office. "I thought I had at least a few minutes of suspended disbelief," she countered.

The chief raised her hands in capitulation. "You're right," she said. "Continue, please."

Mary nodded. "After doing a little investigation and with the help of your department, I was able to narrow down the possibilities of who he was. When he appeared in my office—"

"He traveled to Freeport?" the Chief interrupted. "Did he use a broom?"

Mary merely glanced back at the clock.

"Okay. Okay, continue," the chief said.

"When he was in my office, I was able to show him the report, and he recognized his name," she said. "Then we searched for his son on the Internet, and Steven recognized him. Well, actually he thought his grandson was his son. Then a portion of his memory returned, and he believes he fell down an abandoned mine shaft on his property."

"Mrs. Alden, don't you think the property was checked for mine shafts?" she asked.

Mary shrugged. "Well, I guess you missed it," she said. "I know he's down there."

"Okay, your few minutes are up," she said. "I can't get a warrant to search that property with only a request from you."

"So, what do you need in order to search it?" Mary asked.

"I'd need a request from his family," Chief Chase replied. "So if you can convince them that you're not nuts, we'll take it from there."

The chief stood up.

"Once we get their permission, how long will it take you to get the equipment to search the mine shaft?" Mary asked, standing and looking across the desk at the chief.

"We can get a water department sewer camera out on the property within thirty minutes," she said.

Mary nodded. "Thank you," she said. "And if I were you, I'd let the water department know that you're going to be needing them this afternoon."

"If you're able to get permission that quickly, Mrs. Alden," the chief said, "I'll go out to the property and operate the camera myself."

"Make sure you wear boots," Mary said as she and Bradley left the office.

Chapter Thirty-seven

"You sounded pretty sure in there," Bradley said as he put the key into the cruiser's ignition.

Mary nodded, settled into her seat and put her seatbelt on. "Yeah, I did, didn't I?" she replied. "I sure hope I didn't just put my foot in my mouth."

Bradley shrugged. "It's been in there before," he teased. "You'll get over it."

"Oh, thanks for the vote of confidence," she replied.

"Hey, I'm still here with you," he protested. "I didn't jump up and run out of the office when she thought you were crazy."

"No, you didn't," she agreed, and then she sat up and looked over at him. "But you stayed pretty quiet."

He nodded as he put the car into drive and pulled away from the curb. "Yes, because I knew you could handle yourself, make your point, act like a professional and make me proud," he said. "And you did. I figured anything I said would either detract from what you were saying or make it look like you needed my defending. You didn't. You were amazing."

A little flabbergasted, Mary sat back in her seat and was silent for a few moments. "Well, thank you," she finally said.

Smiling, Bradley turned to her. "You're welcome," he said. "By the way, you're sexy when you're in charge."

Her smile grew into a grin. "Wow, I need you to work with me more often."

Laughing, he pulled to a stop at an intersection. "So, what's next, partner?"

She pulled a notebook from her purse and gave him an address on the other side of Galena. "We need to end up there," she said. "But first, we need to drive over to High Street to see if Steve will come along with me to convince his son to give us permission."

Bradley turned left, drove up the hill to High Street and then turned left again to go back to the location where Mary and Mike had seen Steve several days earlier. He parked the car in the lot next to the Galena Historical Society, and they both got out and walked to the curb. "He was in this area," she said.

She looked up and down the street, but she couldn't see him. Finally, she stepped out onto the street and looked down the hill. "Steve," she called, looking down the hill and waving. "Steve Sonn, is that you?"

Bradley looked around. "Can you see him?" he asked.

Mary looked over her shoulder at him. "No, I can't, but I thought I would look a little less crazy if I pretended I saw someone I knew," she said.

Bradley nodded. "Yeah, that makes sense," he said, and then he walked over to Mary, leaned over her, looked in the same direction and called out. "Steve. Hey Steve, do you have a minute?"

Mary smiled at him. "Thanks."

"No problem," he replied.

"Are you looking for me?" Steve asked, appearing a few feet behind them.

Mary put her hand on Bradley's shoulder and turned him, so he could see Steve.

"Whoa," Bradley said, stepping back instinctively and then lowering his voice, "I understand why you couldn't eat those ribs now. This guy's in bad shape."

"Steve," Mary said. "I need your help."

"What can I do?" he asked.

"In order to do a search to find your body, I need to convince your son, Gregg, to call the police and request the search," she explained.

"Greggie?" he asked, shaking his head. "I don't know. I don't want to bother him, disturb his life."

Frustrated, Mary took a deep breath before she spoke. "Steve, you came to me because you wanted to be found, and the only way we can get you out of that hole is if your son requests that we search the property again," Mary said. "So, you have a choice. Help me talk to your son, or always have him wonder if his dad walked out on him."

"But what if he doesn't believe us? What if he hates me?" Steve cried.

"Then we've both done all we can do," Mary said. "But I think we have to try, for both of you."

Chapter Thirty-eight

A few minutes later, the cruiser pulled up to a modest residential home on the west side of Galena where a man and his son where in the front yard tossing a baseball back and forth. Mary recognized the man as Steve's son, Gregg.

Seeing the cruiser, Gregg held the ball in his glove and turned to his son. "Hey, Stevie, why don't you run inside to Mommy and see if she'll make us some lemonade, okay?"

"Kay, Dad," the six year-old replied.

Turning towards the cruiser, Gregg walked towards the curb. "Hi, can I help you?" he asked.

Mary and Bradley got out of the car and introduced themselves.

"So, I don't understand, why are a Freeport Police Chief and a private investigator here in Galena?" he asked.

"We have some information about your father," Mary said.

She hadn't expected the shocked look on his face. "My father?" he gasped as he sat down on the lawn. "Did you find him? Where has he been?"

Mary knelt down next to him. "Gregg, actually, I need your help to find him," Mary said. "I need you to call Chief Chase and ask her to search your old property."

"We searched the old property," he insisted. "Why should we look again?"

"Because they missed it," she said. "They missed the abandoned mine shaft he fell down."

161

Gregg shook his head. "No, he didn't fall down a mine shaft," he said. "He left us. He was angry with me, something I had done, and he just left us."

"Oh, Greggie," Steve said. "I was never angry with you. I would never leave you."

"Gregg, your dad wasn't mad at you," Mary said. "He loved you. He never would have left you."

Gregg looked up at her, confusion and anger on his face. "How the hell would you know?" he asked. "You've got a lot of nerve to come to my house and act like you know what he was like."

"I don't know what he was like," Mary said. "But I do know what he wants now, and he wants someone to find his body."

He stared at her. "What did you say?"

Mary sighed. "I said he wants his body to be found," she said. "And yes, I know that makes me sound like some kind of a nut. And I can't help that."

Gregg started to stand up and move away from her. "You need to leave," he said. "You need to leave, or I'll call the police."

"Okay, Steve, I need some help here," Mary said.

Gregg stopped. "What did you just say?"

"I asked your dad to give me some help here," Mary said. "He came to me asking me to help him."

"Lady, you are crazy," he said, hurrying towards his house.

"Tell him his favorite book was Curious George, and he made me read it to him every night," Steve said, appearing next to Mary.

"He said your favorite book was Curious George," she called after him. "And you made him read it to you every night."

Gregg stopped and turned. "What?"

162

Mary shrugged. "Curious George," she said.

He came closer. "How did you do that?"

"I wish I could tell you," Mary said. "For some reason ghosts are drawn to me."

"My dad's a ghost?"

"Yes, he's been a ghost for about twenty years," Mary said. "He didn't leave you. He fell down a hole. He tried to get back up, wanted to get back to you and the rest of your family."

"What if I don't believe you?" he asked.

"Well, the only way you can really find out if I'm a fake is to call Chief Chase and search your old property," she said. "If they don't find anything, then you can ask her to arrest me. And believe me, I'm sure she would be delighted to do it."

He pulled his cell phone out of his pocket and called the non-emergency number for the police department. "Hi, this is Gregg Sonn," he said. "I'd like to speak with Chief Chase."

Chapter Thirty-nine

Steve's former house was located up on Prospect Street. It was surrounded by about two acres of land that were partially wooded. Mary and Bradley pulled up just behind the vehicle belonging to the Galena Police Department. Chief Chase stepped out of it and walked to Bradley's cruiser. Mary stepped out to greet the Chief. "Hi," she began.

The Chief shook her head. "No, you listen to me," she said in a lowered voice. "I don't know what you did to convince that poor man to do this, but believe me, if we find a mine shaft, and if we send that camera down and find nothing, I'll not only bring you up on charges but I'll also charge you for the time and equipment used on this wild goose chase."

Mary nodded. "Fair enough," she said. "But you'll have to stand in line. Gregg Sonn has already threatened to file a complaint with you."

Chief Chase just stared at Mary for a few moments, not saying a word, and then she shook her head in disgust and walked away.

Mary felt Bradley's arm around her shoulders and appreciated the squeeze of comfort he gave her. "So, great day to be a ghostbuster, right?" he asked with a tender smile.

"Just make sure we have enough money in the account for bail," she replied. "I might need it."

Bradley turned her towards him. "But Steve's body is down there."

She nodded. "Well, it was…twenty years ago," she explained. "Hopefully rain, flooding and erosion haven't carried it away somewhere."

Leaning forward, he placed a kiss on her forehead. "I'll make sure I have our lawyer's number on speed dial," he whispered.

She giggled. "Thanks."

Mary watched as Chelsea Chase knocked on the door, presented a warrant to the current homeowners and explained the situation. Gregg Sonn stood next to her, introducing himself to the woman on the other side of the door. A moment later they were being ushered through a gate in the fence and into the manicured backyard.

"Wow," Gregg said. "It sure has changed since we lived here. I can barely recognize it."

"Crap," Mary muttered.

She walked away from the group, following the circumference of the back yard. "Um, Steve, it would really be nice for you to show up now," she whispered.

"Okay, Mrs. Alden," Chief Chase called, her arms folded across her chest. "Where's the mine shaft?"

"Just give me a minute," Mary called back, hoping her cheery façade fooled someone in the group.

"Steve," she whispered harshly. "I need you now!"

Appearing next to her, Steve looked around the yard. "Wow, this is nice," he said. "This is really nice. I had hoped to do something like this, but I never got around to it."

"Well, really, I'm sorry," Mary said. "But I'm about to be led off in handcuffs if you don't tell me where the hidden mine shaft is."

Steve looked around again, turning one way and then the other. "Things have really changed since then," he confessed. "And it was such a long time ago."

"You're not boosting my confidence level," she whispered to him and then turned to the waiting group, smiled and called out, "Just getting my bearings."

Steve walked to the very back of the yard where an older fence covered in overgrowth separated the yard from the edge of the bluff. "It's through here," he said, his voice filled with excitement. "I was doing some work on the grade. I remember now."

Walking to the old gate, Mary started to pull away the vines.

"What are you doing?" Gregg asked. "No one ever went out there. Dad said it was off limits."

Mary stopped for a moment and looked over her shoulder. "He was working on the grade," she explained. "That's why he went out here."

Gregg shook his head. "We never looked out here for him," he said. "He always said it was too dangerous."

"For the kids," Steve said. "But I needed to make the repairs."

"It was too dangerous for you kids," Mary repeated. "But he needed to repair some things."

Coming up alongside her, Bradley caught hold of the old gate and, pulling with all his strength, yanked it free from its foliage moorings so they could pass through.

Steve was already on the other side walking the edge of the bluff. Moving to the edge of the property line, he looked out over the view of downtown Galena. "I was here," he said softly. "I remember there was a light breeze and I was enjoying the view. Then I stepped back…"

Mary pointed to the area just behind Steve. "The mine shaft should be right there," she said, moving closer to Steve.

"Oh no you don't," Bradley said, catching her arm and pulling her back. "We don't know how compromised this area is, so let's not step before we check it out."

He turned to one of the men from the Water and Sewer Department. "Do you have anything I can use to prod the ground?" he asked.

"Yeah, I got a two by four in the back of the truck," he replied. "I'll get it."

A few minutes later, with the long two by four in his hands, Bradley punched down against the ground. The first two hits were against solid ground.

"Doesn't look like a mine shaft to me," Chief Chase said.

The third hit nearly threw Bradley off his feet as the end of the board disappeared underneath the sod. He turned to the other chief. "Third time's the charm I guess," he said.

Chapter Forty

Within twenty minutes, the rigging had been set up over the mine shaft, and the fiber optic camera cable was being slowly lowered into the darkness. The monitor displaying the camera's findings showed nothing but limestone with clusters of roots growing out of them. The operator would call out the major depth milestones.

"Twenty feet and nothing," he called.

"It was deeper than that," Mary said, peering at the screen with her fingers crossed. "Keep going."

"Thirty feet," the operator called. "And we're getting pretty close to water."

"Want me to call the lawyer now?" Bradley whispered.

Mary shook her head. "No, he's down there," she said. "We have to find him."

"Thirty-five feet," the operator said, looking up from the rigging. "I don't see nothing down there but mine shaft and water."

"Steve, help me find you," Mary murmured.

"Mary," Steve called from the inside of the shaft, his voice echoing on the stone for Mary's ears only. "Tell him to come down another two feet."

"Could you just lower it down another two feet?" Mary asked.

The operator looked over at the chief for guidance, and she nodded as she rolled her eyes. "Why not?" she said. "We want to be sure that we gave her every chance to prove her theory."

Shrugging, he lowered it a few more feet. "I just got rock," he called out.

"Move the camera to the right…no, no, the left," Steve called. "About a foot over."

"Move the camera over to the left," Mary said. "About a foot over."

"Lady, there ain't going to be nothing…" he began as he slowly moved the camera around. "Well, holy cow. We got ourselves a shelf, just like you said."

Mary took a deep, shuddering breath of relief. "Can you widen the viewer now?" she asked.

He nodded. "Yeah, I'm doing that now," he said, eagerness in his voice. "Okay, what have we got here?"

He looked into the monitor, then paused and sat up. "Chief, I think you need to look at this," he said.

"He found me," Steve said, appearing next to Mary. "He found my body."

Chief Chase hurried over to the monitor and studied it for a moment. She gave Mary a puzzled look but then turned her attention to Gregg. "I believe we've found the remains of your father," she said softly. "Would you care to look?"

Tears forming in his eyes, he hurried over to stare into the monitor. "He didn't leave us," he whispered, looking over his shoulder at Mary. "He never left us."

"He did all he could to climb out," Mary said. "He wanted to get back to you. But he only got as far as the shelf."

"Could you tell him I love him?" Steve asked, placing his arm around his son's shoulders.

Gregg's eyes widened, and he tentatively looked around. "I love you too, Dad," he whispered before Mary could say a word. "I love you, too."

Chapter Forty-one

Bradley placed his arm around his wife's shoulders and walked her back to the cruiser. "That was amazing," he said. "I loved the look on Chief Chase's face when she looked through the monitor. It was a cross between disbelief and horror."

Mary looked up at him and smiled. "Well, now she has to believe in ghosts," she said. "That can be a little disconcerting."

He unlocked the car and opened her door. "Is there anything else we have to do here?" he asked.

She shook her head as she climbed into the car. "No. After Gregg told his dad he loved him, Steve was more than happy to move on," she said. "And the police department will deal with removing his earthly remains."

"How about Gregg?" Bradley asked.

"I think he needs a little time to get his head around all this," Mary said. "I gave him my card, so he can contact me when he's ready."

He closed her door and entered on the other side. With the key in the ignition, he turned to her. "So, can we go home and relax?" he asked. "It's been a fairly eventful day."

"Sorry," she said, shaking her head. "But tonight my mom gets into town, and Rosie and Stanley are coming to dinner."

Bradley took a deep breath and then smiled. "Well, being with family can be relaxing," he said. "Besides, I have this need to hug Clarissa and let her know I love her."

"Yeah, I don't think kids can hear that too many times," she agreed.

They went directly home and pulled up in the driveway about forty-five minutes later. Clarissa ran out to the porch to meet them. "Guess what?" she called as she hurried down the steps and across the lawn. "Grandma and Grandpa have a present for me. But Grandma said I couldn't see it until you got home."

Bradley picked her up and hugged her. "Well, let's go see what they got you," he said.

Clarissa leaned over, hugged Mary and then studied her. "You have mud all over your shirt," she said.

Mary nodded. "Yeah, I got splashed by a mud puddle."

"So was this an unlucky day?" she asked.

Shaking her head, Mary leaned up and gave her a kiss. "No, sweetheart, this was a very lucky day."

They entered the house, and Mary's mother, Margaret, enfolded them all in a big hug. "Well, I'm going to apologize for your father," she said. "I have no idea what he was thinking, but, well, that's an O'Reilly man for you. Let your heart do the thinking for you and consider the consequences later."

Bradley smiled. "I don't think just the O'Reilly men have that problem," he said.

Margaret looked at her daughter and smiled. "Well, yes, you have the right of that, Bradley," she agreed. "It's a curse for anyone with the O'Reilly name."

"So what did Da do that is so terrible?" she asked.

"Well the gift he sent is not the usual kind of gift one sends to your granddaughter," she said. "But

171

he said, seeing as the party was going to be on Friday the Thirteenth, we needed a good luck charm to be on our side."

"A good luck charm?" Mary asked. "What kind of good luck charm?"

Margaret walked over to the kitchen table and picked up a fairly large box with a lid. "This kind," she said, placing it on the floor.

Clarissa, her eyes wide with excitement, turned to her parents. "Can I open it?" she asked.

"Go ahead," Bradley said, "so we can see what kind of trouble your grandfather is going to be in."

Clarissa lifted the lid and peered inside. "Oh. Oh. Oh!" she cried, reaching down into the box. "It's perfect; it's what I always wanted."

She pulled her hands out, and in them was a tiny, black kitten.

"A kitten?" Mary asked, watching her daughter cuddle it to her chest. "He got her a kitten?"

Margaret sighed and nodded her head. "He found it when he was on patrol, in a sack by the river," she explained, her expression tightening with anger for a moment. "The mother and litter mates didn't make it. So, here was this tiny speck of black fur, he tells me, that needed a home and someone to love it. And besides, he says, it has to be good luck."

Mary stroked the kitten with her finger, and it purred loudly. "Well, you can never have too much good luck," Mary said.

"We can keep it?" Clarissa asked, her face filled with hope.

Mary looked up at Bradley. "Well?"

"Well, we really can't risk giving good luck away," he said, dropping a kiss on the top of Clarissa's head. "What are you going to call it?"

"Lucky," Clarissa said immediately, placing her cheek against the soft fur. "Because it's lucky for us and lucky for the kitten."

"Perfect," Mary said. "Just perfect."

Chapter Forty-two

It was Mary's turn to say goodnight to Clarissa. She and Bradley had learned that if each of them took turns with her, she was able to share different concerns with each of them as they had some one on one time with her. Clarissa was nearly asleep, the tiny kitten snuggled into her pillow purring loudly.

"This has been the best day ever," a sleepy Clarissa yawned. "I love Lucky."

"And it seems that she loves you right back," Mary said, stroking the kitten. "I think it was very lucky indeed that Grandpa found her, for both of you."

Clarissa nodded happily. "I'm never going to believe in bad luck again," she said decisively. "Lucky is a black cat, and she is just perfect."

"Yes she is," Mary agreed. "Just like you."

They sat in silence for a moment, and then Clarissa turned in her bed and looked at Mary. "Is your job dangerous?" she asked, a wrinkle line of worry appearing on her forehead.

Pondering for a moment before she responded, Mary debated whether truth was better than peace of mind. "Well, most of the time my job is very safe," she said. "I research things on my computer. I talk to people and I help solve problems. But there are circumstances that are riskier than others, so for those times I make sure I take precautions and am very careful."

"But it's dangerous?" Clarissa repeated.

Mary nodded. "Yes, sometimes it can be dangerous. Why do you ask?"

"Mrs. Fuller from down the street was visiting Mrs. Brennan today," Clarissa said. "We were playing, so she didn't think we were listening."

Mary shook her head. Children, she had learned, were always listening.

"She said that she wondered how you and Daddy could both have such dangerous jobs," Clarissa continued. "How you could risk your lives when you had a child at home to take care of."

"Well, what do you think about what she said?" Mary asked, knowing that was the only important part of this conversation.

"Sometimes I get scared that I'm going to be alone again," Clarissa admitted. "That you and Daddy are going to die."

Mary placed her hand on Clarissa's head and gently stroked her hair. "Those are pretty scary thoughts, aren't they?" she asked. "Should we think about some other things that might make you feel better when you have those kinds of thoughts?"

"What kind of things?" she asked.

"Well, let's see," Mary replied. "First, let's talk about the 'you being alone again' part. Did you know that your daddy and I have talked to a lawyer and have made a plan that if anything ever happens to us, you will not be alone?"

Clarissa shook her head.

"Well, we have a list of people whom we have asked to take care of you in case that ever happens," Mary said. "Your grandparents are on that list, your Uncle Sean, the Brennans, Stanley and Rosie, and even Ian."

"Ian?" Clarissa asked. "Even he would take care of me?"

"He said he was honored that we asked him," Mary said and then added in her best Ian accent, "and he would take his little darling and protect her with his life."

Clarissa smiled broadly. "I love Ian."

Mary laughed and placed a kiss on Clarissa's forehead. "Now, don't get any ideas about leaving us for Ian," she teased. "And, of course, you have Mike who is your guardian angel, and he will be there to watch over you and protect you. And he loves you very much."

She smiled contentedly. "I love Mike, too," she said.

"So now, let's talk about the dangerous part," Mary said. "Both your father and I have been trained to do our jobs. Most days our jobs are just about helping people, but some days we have to deal with bad people. Then it's a little trickier. But, we are very careful. We don't take risks because we have a sweet daughter waiting for us at home, and we want her to be safe with us."

Clarissa yawned again, her body relaxing into her bed. "So, I'm safe, and you're safe," she whispered, her eyes slowly closing.

"Exactly, sweetheart," Mary whispered back. "I love you."

"I love you, too," she murmured sleepily.

Mary kissed her once more then stood and walked over to the door. "Goodnight, pumpkin," she said, turning off the light.

"Night, Mom," was the soft, nearly inaudible response.

Mary stepped outside the bedroom and closed the door softly.

"Nice job," Mike whispered as he appeared next to her.

"Thanks," she replied. "It's hard being a child, isn't it?"

Mike nodded. "But I bet it's just as hard being a parent."

She shook her head, thinking about all the "parents" Liza had encountered over her short life. "No, it's not hard being a parent," she said. "It's hard being a good parent. But it's worth it."

Chapter Forty-three

"How's she doing?" Bradley asked, meeting her at the foot of the stairs.

"Well, she had some questions about our jobs," Mary said. "Mrs. Fuller visited Katie today and expressed her concern about both of us having such dangerous jobs with a child at home."

"Isn't it nice to have a neighbor who cares enough about your business to share it with others?" Margaret asked with a smile.

"Well, she could have just been concerned," Mary said.

"Aye, and if she were really concerned, she would have come to see you and expressed her worry, not your neighbor," Margaret replied. "What she wanted was a wee bit of gossip to go with her tea."

"So, how's Clarissa?" Bradley asked. "Should I go up there and talk to her?"

Mary placed her hand on Bradley's arm and stopped him from dashing up the stairs. "She's fine. Actually, she was just falling off to sleep when I left her," she said. "I told her that she would never be alone again, even if something were to happen to us. I let her know who we'd listed as potential guardians for her and reminded her that Mike would always be there for her."

She smiled at Bradley. "Although we might have to worry about her trading us in for a flashier, sexier, Scottish model," she said.

"So, you told her Ian was on the list," Bradley chuckled.

"Don't see what that foreigner's got that I don't got," Stanley muttered from across the room.

Rosie secretly winked at Mary and Bradley, and then turned to Stanley. "Neither do I, sweetheart," she reassured him. "Neither do I."

"And then I told her that our jobs were mostly about helping people, but sometimes they could be dangerous," Mary added. "But when they are, we take special care."

"Speaking of special care," Margaret inserted, "Bradley was just telling us about the raid tomorrow morning."

Expecting a lecture, Mary inhaled swiftly, turned and smiled at her mother. "Yes?" she asked, praying inwardly for patience.

"If it's fine with you, I thought I'd spend the day with Clarissa, perhaps take her out to breakfast," her mother suggested. "And if you're with Bradley, I'd love to drive your Roadster. That way neither of us will be sitting around worrying about you."

Gratitude filled her heart, and blinking back tears, she crossed the room and slipped onto the couch next to her mother and into her arms. "Thank you, Mom," she said.

"Ah, there's my girl," her mother crooned, comforting her adult child. "You're doing a fine job being a mother. You handled Clarissa's concerns perfectly. I'm proud of you."

Lifting up her head, she sent her mom a watery smile. "I'm so emotional right now," she confessed, wiping her cheeks. "I cry at the drop of a hat."

"It was the same with me," her mother said. "You're father got so used to it, one time before we had a conversation he pulled a pile of tissues out of the box and handed them to me."

Mary chuckled. "And how did that go over?" she asked.

"I threw the tissues, the box and a few other things at the big, insensitive lout," she replied with a laugh. "And then I cried, and he brought me more tissues."

"Men," Rosie said.

"Exactly," Mary and Margaret agreed.

Bradley turned to Stanley. "What do you say we go do the dishes or something safe like that?" he suggested.

Looking around at the women and then back at Bradley, he nodded. "Yeah, being a husband is a dangerous job iffen you ask me."

Chapter Forty-four

Gigi poured herself another glass of scotch and tossed it down, delicately wiping the excess from the corners of her mouth. "You did well today, Joey," she said, placing the shot glass down next to the half-full bottle. "And by that I mean you weren't your usual, incompetent self."

Giggling, she tottered sideways and quickly righted herself by grabbing hold of the back of an overstuffed chair. Holding tightly, she followed it around and finally slipped into it, laying her legs over the arms. "I'm in such a good mood, Joey," she said, kicking her feet and lifting her arms over her head in a stretch. "Such a great mood."

Suddenly, she turned to him and smiled. "Find me something to kill, okay Joey?"

It was nearly midnight, and Joey had driven back and forth to Quincy that day, a total of about seven hours of driving. He was sitting on the couch in his boxers and a t-shirt with a bottle of beer in his hand, and he didn't want to go out.

"Gigi, darling," he said. "We don't have anything for you to kill. We'll have to go out tomorrow and get something new."

"How about goats?" she asked. "We got goats, right?"

He shook his head. "No, you took care of them last week, remember?" he said. "You got upset about something and went out and killed all four of them."

She sighed. "Oh, yeah, I remember," she said. "And I did it so fast it wasn't even fun."

"Well, tomorrow we'll have the new little girl," he enticed. "And that will be so much fun."

She sighed and dropped her feet down. "It's not that fun," she said. "You get to do all the fun parts. All I get to do is watch and film. It would be so much more fun to get my hands on her."

Turning again, a smile of desire in her eyes, she looked at Joey. "How about if we change places tomorrow?" she asked. "You could film, and I could have fun?"

"Well, sweetie, what do you think our viewers would think of that?" he asked, knowing the answer. "Would they like a little woman on girl sport?"

Shaking her head, she sighed. "No, the bastards, they like to pretend they're you," she complained. "They'd be furious."

She turned away from Joey and pressed her head into the back cushions of the chair. "Joey," she whimpered. "Can we get some kittens next week?"

"Yes, darling," he said. "I'll check in the free papers and see if there are any being offered."

She turned around to look at him again. "Can't we just go to the pound again?"

He shook his head. "No, darling, they are getting suspicious," he said. "We've adopted our limit with them."

"Why do people have to be so suspicious?" she cried petulantly. "Why don't they just let us do what we want?"

"Perhaps we could leave for Quincy a little early tomorrow and see if they have an animal shelter," Joey suggested.

She scooted around in the chair, wrapping her arms around her legs and slowly rocking back and forth in the chair. "Oh, Joey, that would be so fun," she said, her words gently slurring together. "You would do that for me?"

Joey stood up, walked across the room to her chair and helped her up. "Of course I would do that for you," he said as he wrapped his arm around her waist and guided her toward their bedroom. "You know I would do anything for you."

She cuddled into him. "Thank you, Joey," she said. "And, if you want, after we kill the little girl, you can help me kill the kitten."

Chapter Forty-five

The predawn activity in the parking lot at the Jo Daviess County Courthouse was as low profile as possible, with vehicles from various local law enforcement agencies quietly pulling into the parking spaces and their occupants discreetly walking from the vehicles to the basement door that led to a small conference room.

Coffee and donuts seemed to be the mainstay of most law enforcement missions, and this one was like countless others Mary had participated in. She skipped the coffee, opting instead for a carton of milk, and then walked over to peruse the donuts, hoping for a chocolate glazed, Bavarian-cream-filled, long john.

Just as she spotted one and picked up a napkin to reach for it, a familiar voice rang out behind her. "What the hell is she doing here?"

Mary grabbed the donut and turned to face Chief Chase, who was not, by any stretch, happy to see her.

"Morning, Chief," Mary said politely. "Good to see you again."

"You do know that being married to a law enforcement official does not make you an honorary member of the team," she said.

Ouch, Mary thought. No wonder Mike never called you back.

"Wow, thanks," Mary replied. "I'll have to let Bradley know."

She glanced around to find her husband and saw him speaking with Chris Thorne, the FBI agent who was leading the raid. "I'll tell him as soon as he's done meeting with Chris," Mary said with another pleasant smile. "Have a donut. It seems like you could use the sugar."

She was just about to walk away when Chris called everyone to attention. "I want to thank you all for agreeing to work with us today," he said. "Our number one priority is to stop an international child pornography source. We not only need to arrest the suspects but we also need to conduct a thorough search throughout the compound to discover and confiscate evidence."

There was a quick wave of surprised murmurs as local law enforcement heard that something as diabolical as a child pornography source was within their borders. Chris allowed them a moment and then called them back to order. "I'd like to give some time to the person whose investigation has led us to the best lead we've had in years," Chris said. "I'd like to introduce you to a former, decorated, Chicago police officer and now a law enforcement consultant, Mary O'Reilly Alden."

Mary sent an apologetic grimace towards Chief Chase. "I'll mention something to Chris, too," she murmured before walking to the front of the room, leaving a slightly astonished chief of police in her wake.

"Thank you, Chris," she said when she got to the front of the room. "I'm going to just take a quick minute to give you an overview of the situation. We have a couple who have posed as a minister and his wife. Several independent sources will testify that these two have been culpable in the re-homing or underground adoption of a number of female children. We know of at least two situations where the child has been used in a live web stream of a pornographic nature and then, during the broadcast, murdered. These snuff films are not only illegal but also brutal and unconscionable. Our source tells us that there is a barn behind the main house that has been converted to a high-tech film studio. We are hoping there is some evidence out there including computer hard drives, DNA evidence and props for the films. We also have information that many of the children have been buried in the woods behind the barn. So once the area is secure, we should bring in forensics to identify the bodies."

The room was totally silent, each man and woman reaching into their training and experience to mentally prepare for the raid. They had no idea exactly what they would be walking into, and they didn't want to be surprised.

"Are there any questions?" Mary asked.

Chief Chase raised her hand. "Who are your sources?" she asked, a hint of skepticism in her voice.

Mary met her eyes, understanding the challenge. "I'm sorry," she said evenly. "Because of the risk involved with this case, the names have to be kept confidential."

Chief Chase kept her eyes trained on Mary and shook her head slightly enough that Mary knew she wasn't satisfied with the answer, but for the sake of the assignment, she wouldn't say anything else.

Chris stepped up, gave everyone a copy of the address, an aerial view of the property and divided the group into two teams, one that would go into the house and the other into the barn. "Once again, I'm grateful to you for your willingness to work with the FBI on this raid," Chris said. "I'll be lead car, followed by Chief Alden from Freeport. My car will lead Team A to the house; Alden will lead Team B to the barn. Be alert, be smart and be safe. Let's go."

Chapter Forty-six

Mary and Bradley hurried to their car only to find Chelsea Chase waiting next to it. "I've got a number of my guys going out on this raid," she said. "I need to know if this is another one of your psychic games."

"It's not a game," Mary replied seriously, "and I would never put law enforcement agents in jeopardy without good cause. I get that you have an issue with me, and that's fine. But right now, we've got a job to do. If you're not comfortable with the raid, pull out now. Just let Chris know."

"I'm not pulling out," Chief Chase said. "I'm just not going to let you get my guys killed."

She abruptly turned away before Mary could respond.

"She's doesn't like you very much, does she?" Bradley calmly asked.

Mary shook her head. "No, we're okay," she said as she climbed into the cruiser. "But I think I pissed her off when I took that last filled long john."

Bradley chuckled softly. "Really? Are you okay?" he asked.

"Yeah, actually, I'm better than okay," she said. "I'm ready to kick some butt."

Bradley pulled the cruiser out of the parking spot and pulled up behind Chris's vehicle. "Don't let her bother you," he said. "She doesn't understand what you do, and that frightens her. And she doesn't like feeling that way."

Shaking her head, Mary sat back in the seat. "I'm not letting her bother me," Mary admitted. "I actually admire her. She's worried about her officers, and she's willing to confront me so they're safe. I can respect and admire that."

Chris pulled out onto the street, and Bradley followed. Mary peered into the side mirror to watch the caravan of vehicles follow them down the streets of Galena. "We've got a good-sized group. There's got to be eighteen of us," Mary said. "Don't you think this is overkill?"

"I'd rather have too many than too few," he said. "And the more people around, the greater protection for you."

"Bradley, you need to concentrate on the job, not me," she said. "We both know that if your mind's not on the raid, it's dangerous."

"Besides, I'll be watching out for her," Mike said from the backseat of the car.

Both Mary and Bradley jumped. "I really hate when you do that," Mary said.

"So, how did the briefing go?" Mike asked.

"Good," Bradley replied. "But your old girlfriend isn't too fond of Mary."

"Well, that's understandable," Mike said.

"Excuse me?" Mary asked.

"Well, it's obvious she never got over me," Mike said, "and her discovering that I'm hanging out with you is making her jealous. Really, Mary, I thought you'd see that right away."

Grinning, Bradley glanced over at Mary. "Yes, Mary, you should have seen that," he teased. "I'm surprised she didn't jump up and try to pull your hair."

"Mike, I don't know if both you and your ego can fit in the backseat of this car," Mary replied.

"Good thing we're almost there," Bradley said, the teasing tone leaving his voice. "Okay, when we get out, Mary, I want you to try to make contact with Bill Patterson's ghost. Mike, you stay with Mary."

"I'm guessing Bill will find me as soon as we're on the property," Mary said. "He said he'd keep an eye out for us, and I have a feeling he'll be anxious to help."

"Okay, so once we're in, see if Bill can show you some of those hidden panels he mentioned," Bradley said. "I would guess that's where the most damning information is going to be hidden."

Mary nodded. "Okay, where will you be?"

"Covering you while you search," he said, "and directing the other officers to areas in the barn you aren't searching."

"Good idea," she said. "So, I can have a conversation with Bill without worrying about freaking anyone else out."

The car in front of them slowed, and Bradley pressed his brake. He took a deep breath and looked over at Mary. "I love you," he said, reaching over and grasping her hand.

She smiled at him. "I love you, too," she replied, squeezing his hand in response.

"Be careful," he admonished.

"You, too," she said.

He turned the car and followed Chris into the driveway leading to the house.

Chapter Forty-seven

"Joey, get your ass out of bed!" Gigi screamed as she ran to their closet and pulled out a handgun.

"What?" Joey muttered, sitting up in the bed and rubbing his eyes. "What's wrong?"

"A raid," Gigi screamed, tossing another handgun on the bed. "We've got a bunch of cops coming up the driveway."

Immediately awake, Joey jumped out of bed and grabbed the gun. "How many?"

"Looks like five, maybe six vehicles," she said. "I can't see how many are in each. What do you think I am, psychic?"

"We've got to give up," Joey cried. "We're never going to be able to beat six vehicles filled with cops. We'd need an army."

Gigi went back to the closet, pulled out a semi-automatic rifle, slapped a magazine into it and then tossed another magazine on the desk. "We got an army," she said. "Now get your chicken ass out of bed and be a man for once. There are 30 rounds in this rifle and 30 more on the desk. There's no way they got 60 cops out there, so you've got plenty of ammunition."

"Listen, Gigi, we're not Bonnie and Clyde," he pleaded. "There's no way we can kill a whole bunch of cops and get away with it."

She looked at him in disgust. "You know who my daddy is," she spat. "One call from him, and we are sailing to Venezuela with a bank account full of money and new identities. We can set up shop anywhere we want. Now grab the gun."

He took a deep shuddering breath. "You sure?" he asked her, sliding out of the bed and picking up the gun. "You sure we can do this?"

She rolled her eyes. "Have I ever been wrong before?" she asked.

She glanced up at the security cameras and saw that the cars were nearly to the end of the drive. "Okay, I'm going to run over to the barn and grab the vendor list and the hard drive. The rest of the stuff is expendable," she said. "You meet the company. I'll take the tunnel, so I'll be back and forth as fast as I can."

"You hate that dark tunnel," Joey said.

"Yeah, but this time, it's the safest and the quickest way to get over there," she said, and for the first time that morning, a slight smile appeared on her face. "And if I'm lucky, a cop or two will be in the barn so I can get a little target practice in."

She looked down at the gun in her hand and then back up at Joey, an entirely different look in her eyes. Grabbing the second gun on the bed, she stuffed it into the pocket of her robe. "This is going to be a great morning," she said. "Now, let's get the furniture arranged before I leave."

They walked over to the large overstuffed couch. "We need to drop this onto its back," she said, "so you can hide behind it and fire at them when they come through the door."

"But won't they be able to see me?" he asked.

"We'll turn the lights off," she said. "You'll have the advantage. Now help me with this damn couch."

The couch dropped, and Joey knelt behind it, the rifle next to his shoulder and his eye at the viewer. "I'm ready, Gigi," he said. "I'm ready for some action."

"Yeah, for the first time in your life," she muttered.

"What?" he asked nervously. "What did you say?"

"I said you look good," she lied. "And you are going to take them all down. Just aim at the doorway and keep shooting. I'll be back as soon as I can."

Gigi quickly turned off all of the lights in the house and moved to the kitchen. "I'll be back as soon as I can," she repeated. "Are you okay?"

"Yeah, I'm good. I can hear them coming, so go, Gigi. Go now," he called and he rested his finger against the trigger.

Grabbing a flashlight from a hook in the kitchen, Gigi opened the pantry door and went to the far end of the small, closet-like room. Pushing on a hidden panel, the back of the pantry popped open to reveal a set of stairs. She turned on the flashlight, stepped down onto the first stair and pulled the door closed behind her.

The air felt cool and smelled of wet dirt. Grabbing onto the handrail, she pointed the flashlight so it only pointed down and continued down the short flight of wooden stairs to the beginning of the tunnel. Once Gigi could feel the damp earth against her bare feet, she shined the flashlight around the space, shuddering at the exposed roots that seemed like fingers reaching out from the ground to grab her. The barn was nearly thirty yards away.

She hated the feeling of dirt all around her, closing her in. It felt like she was in her own grave. She hesitated for a moment, and then she heard a volley of gunshots from behind her and realized she had to hurry. If she and Joey were going to escape, she needed to get their records from the barn. Taking a deep breath, she stepped forward and started to run towards the doorway on the other side of the tunnel, the doorway that led into the barn.

Chapter Forty-eight

Bradley drove past Chris's car and the house to get to the barn. He waited until the other two cars in his group joined him, and then they all got out at the same time. Chief Chase climbed out of the car next to them. Bradley nodded to her and all the others in the group. "Weapons drawn," he whispered. "We don't know what we are walking into."

Mary adjusted her Kevlar vest, pulled her revolver from her holster and fell into line with the other members of her team. She hated the fact that Bradley led the way into the barn, but she realized that was one of the responsibilities of being the team leader. Bradley waited until everyone was ready to go in before giving the nod to proceed. Mary held to the back of the line and covertly looked around.

"Looking for someone?" Chief Chase asked her.

Mary nodded. "Well, if you must know, I'm looking for a dead contractor who is going to show me where he built the hidden panels in the barn," she replied.

Shaking her head with disgust, Chief Chase moved around Mary. "You are certifiable and you don't belong here. You're going to get someone killed."

Mary looked around again, searching for Bill. She couldn't believe he wouldn't show up. The rest of the team had already entered the barn and begun the search. She couldn't wait for Bill any longer. Moving towards the barn, she suddenly she heard a volley of gunshots coming from the house. She turned around, weapon drawn, and faced the house. Mike appeared next to her. "You need to get into the barn," he said.

She shook her head, focused on the house. "They've got return fire in there," she said.

"Mary," he said, standing in front of her. "They have enough backup. They should be fine. You've got an assignment."

Mary hesitated for a moment.

"Mary," Mike said. "We need to find the hidden panels.

She nodded and stepped backwards towards the barn, her eyes still on the house. "Okay, let's go."

When she crossed the threshold of the barn, she saw Bill waiting just inside the door. "Come on," he said, pointing to a corner of the barn. "The hidden panels are over here."

Mary looked around the barn. The other members of the team were systematically searching the other side of the room. There would be sixty feet between her and the areas they would be searching, plenty of room for privacy.

Running, Mary followed Bill to the far end of the barn where a room had been constructed near one of the corners. "This is the control room," Bill said. "It's where all the computer stuff is, and it's also where the panels are hidden."

Mary reached down, her hand clasped on the doorknob when she felt a hand on her shoulder. "What are you doing?" Chief Chase asked.

Where the hell did she come from? Mary wondered.

"I'm searching this room," Mary replied, fed up with the chief's treatment. "And I don't have the time or inclination to explain my actions to you. So, if you'll excuse me…"

Mary started to twist the door knob open when she heard a soft click from the area just past the room. "Bill?" she called.

"Damn it, Mary, I forgot about the secret panel," he cried. "Someone's coming through."

"Down!" Mary yelled, dropping down to the floor.

"Why?" Chief Chase asked. "Did one of your dead friends—"

A six foot panel popped open, and Gigi jumped out, her gun drawn. "Die!" she screamed as she jumped into the light. Chief Chase started to turn, but it was too late. Gigi had picked her closest target, and the chief was in her sights.

Mary watched the chief's eyes widen in shock when the bullet hit. Its impact knocked her forward past Mary and into the outer wall of the control room. It seemed like everything was happening in slow motion. Mary turned to see Gigi raise her gun again, aiming it across the room at another officer. Without thinking, Mary raised her weapon and fired. The shot crashed against the side of Gigi's gun and tore it from her hands.

Gigi glanced over at Mary, studied her momentarily and then dashed back into the tunnel.

Mary looked back over her shoulder and saw the smear of red blood on the white enamel wall left by Chief Chase as she slid to the floor.

"I've got her," Mike yelled.

Mary got to her feet. "I'm going after her," she yelled to Mike, her police training kicking in. "I can't let her get away."

She dove into the tunnel, sticking close to the wall, and started following Gigi.

"Mary," Bradley yelled from the entrance. "Mary, are you okay?"

She turned and could see his dark silhouette in the opening. A shot rang out past Mary and ricocheted off one of the support beams near the exit. "Get down!" she yelled.

"Mary!" Bradley called.

"Bradley, I'm fine," she yelled back. "Get out of her line of sight. Chase has been shot. She needs an ambulance, ASAP!"

The tunnel curved slightly, and Mary was enveloped in darkness except for the bobbing flashlight of the woman she was following. "Stop! Police!" Mary called. "We've got you cornered."

Another shot ricocheted wildly and struck another beam. Mary hugged the dirt wall and continued down the tunnel in the dark.

"Mary, it's Bill," the ghost called.

She couldn't see him, but she her skin chilled at his presence. "I can hear you," she whispered.

"You got to get out of here," he said. "We never finished this tunnel. We only put in a couple temporary supports. The ground is too unstable. It's sandy soil, and with the echoing of the gunshots, it could come down at any moment."

"I can't let her surprise the guys on the other side," she said.

"Then make her come back," Bill suggested. "Shoot out her flashlight. This side is closer, and she don't like being in the tunnel."

Mary moved to the middle of the tunnel, making sure there was no light behind her, and aimed for the far edge of the flashlight. Taking a quick breath, she squeezed the trigger and fired. A moment later the tunnel was completely dowsed in blackness.

"You bitch!" Gigi screamed. "I'm going to kill you."

"I won't shoot you," Mary called, "if you just give up and come back this way. It's not safe in here. The tunnel could collapse."

Gigi fired another shot and Mary heard it thump into the dirt wall only a few feet away. Then she heard the rumble.

"Mary, get out!" Bill screamed. "It's coming down!"

She turned and started to run. The ground beneath her feet started to shake, and she was tossed against the wall. Trying to get her bearings in the darkness, she called out. "Which way?"

"Mary, this way!" Bradley called from behind her.

Following his voice, she stumbled forward as clumps of dirt began to drop from the ceiling. Another shot rang out somewhere behind her, and she felt the tunnel reverberate in response. Finally, she reached the curve where she could see the opening. She placed her foot forward to run, but suddenly the walls on either side of her collapsed. "Bradley," she started to cry out as she reached for him, but her words were cut off by a layer of soft soil.

A tiny pocket of air had formed beneath her face when she protected her face with her arm. Her other arm had been extended and was trapped in the dirt. She breathed shallowly, trying not to panic. Bradley saw where she was. He was only a few yards away. The tunnel couldn't be that deep. She took a short shuddering breath and prayed. "Oh, God, please don't let me die. Please save my baby."

She felt pressure on her extended hand. Someone was clasping it. Suddenly, she felt herself being pulled up out of the dirt. She gasped deeply when the air hit her face, and a moment later, she was pulled into Bradley's embrace.

"Damn it," he whispered hoarsely. "You scared me to death."

She took in another deep, shuddering breath. "I scared me to death, too," she gasped. "Thanks for pulling me out."

"It wasn't that hard," he said. "This part of the tunnel was only a half foot from the ground, so when I came running out here, I could see your fingers in the sand."

"How about Gigi?" she asked.

"She's down there, somewhere, about four feet under," he said. "We've got guys digging, but I don't know if she's going to be so lucky."

Bradley led her back into the barn, and they hurried back to Chief Chase, watching the EMTs work on her. Mike was kneeling over her, offering encouraging words. "Chelsea, hang in there," he urged.

Chelsea's eyes fluttered open for a moment. "Mike? Mike is that you?" she asked, her voice weak and disoriented. "Are you going to walk me home?"

He shook his head. "I hope not, sweetheart," he whispered. "I hope not."

Mary could see the bullet entrance wound had caused a hole below her shoulder that oozed blood, and she knew that exit wound was going to be even worse.

"Let's pray the bullet missed her heart," she murmured.

The EMTs carefully lifted her and placed her on the gurney. With her IV waving as they pushed her away, they rushed her out of the barn and to the waiting ambulance.

"Mary, she could see me," Mike said, appearing next to her. "She wanted me to walk her home."

"No," Mary said stubbornly. "She is not going home. She's staying here."

Chapter Forty-nine

The ambulance pulled out of the driveway and flew down the road towards Galena, its siren screaming. A moment later, a handcuffed Joey was guided out of the house to a waiting squad car. Chris walked over to join Mary and Bradley on the lawn in front of the house.

"He was hiding behind the couch in the living room with a semi-automatic rifle, waiting for us," Chris said. "When we burst in, he let loose a volley of shots. But what he didn't plan on was the kickback of the gun. The first shots went wild, and the next ones ended up in the ceiling. By the time he scrambled off his back, we were across the room, guns drawn, and he gave up without a fight."

Another ambulance pulled into the driveway and drove past them and the long narrow ditch that was filled with men and shovels.

"What happened there?" Chris asked.

"There was a tunnel from the house to the barn," Mary said, taking a deep breath to steady herself. "A female gunman jumped out with her gun drawn and shot the first person she saw, Police Chief Chase."

"How's Chase doing?" he asked.

Bradley put his arm around Mary and squeezed her lightly to comfort her. "The EMTs worked on her for a while," he said. "They were able to stabilize her before they put her in the ambulance, so that's a good sign. But it was a bad looking wound."

"So what happened to you?" he asked Mary.

"The gunman ran back into the tunnel," Bradley answered. "So of course, my wife had to follow."

"I didn't want her jumping out on the other end, surprising you," she said.

"Well, thank you," he said. "She would have had the jump on us, because once we searched the premises for anyone else, we read Joey his Miranda rights and started asking questions."

He brushed some of the dirt from Mary's shoulder. "So, then what happened?"

"The tunnel collapsed," Mary said. "I was nearly at the opening."

"Not nearly enough," Bradley inserted. "Luckily, closer to the barn, the tunnel was only inches below the dirt, so I could pull her out. We're still searching for the gunman's body. We don't know where she was in the tunnel, and nearer to the house the tunnel is closer to eight feet underground."

Chris nodded and looked at Mary. "Do you want to follow Chief Chase to the hospital?" he asked.

Mary shook her head. "No, we sent one of her guys with her," she said, reassured knowing Mike had gone along with them too.

"I didn't mean to watch over her," Chris said with a smile. "I meant would you like to go to the hospital to be checked over?"

She shook her head. "I hate hospitals," she said. "Besides, we want to find the evidence to shut this place down."

"Okay," Chris said, moving past them towards the barn. "Let's go."

Bill was waiting inside when Mary walked back into the barn. "I won't be sorry if Gigi's dead," he said. "Does that make me a bad person?"

Mary shook her head. "No, that makes you human," she replied quietly. "Now, let's find those panels so we can get out of here. This place gives me the creeps."

In a matter of minutes, Mary had called some of Chris's technicians over to the control room to collect several files filled with information and the hard drive.

"This is great," Chris said. "How did you find these panels so quickly?"

"Mary has a sixth sense about these things," Bradley said.

Chris smiled. "I don't know if I mentioned it," he said. "But I worked with your brother Sean a couple months ago and he told me this amazing story about his kid sister."

Mary sighed softly. She really didn't feel like being judged again. "Yeah, I know what you're thinking," she said, her voice tired.

"Really?" he asked. "Because I was raised in an old house that was definitely haunted. I've seen a number of ghosts in my day. I have no problem believing what Sean told me."

"Thank you," she said. "It gets a little exhausting either having to hide what you can do or justifying it to people who don't believe no matter how well you perform."

He nodded. "Yeah, I can imagine," he said. "Now, I know it's been a really a long morning, but I was wondering if you and Bradley wanted to take a walk in the woods with me so I could make a list of some of the names of the buried."

Bradley nodded. "It makes it a lot easier to identify bodies if you know who you're looking for," he said.

"That's my thinking," Chris replied.

"Sure, I can do that," Mary said. "The first two people you need to put on your list are Liza Parker, a five-year-old who had been adopted by the Larson family in Dubuque, Iowa. We can send you the contact information."

Mary looked over to Bill Patterson, who had been standing next to them the whole time they'd been speaking. "And the next is Bill Patterson, a contractor from Dubuque," she said. "He was the source who told us about the barn and what happened here. He told me about the secret tunnel and probably saved my life. He's a true hero, and it would be nice if his family knew about his heroism."

Chris jotted down the name. "I'll make sure I personally handle this one," he said.

"Thank you," Mary replied.

"Thank you, Mary," Bill said. "Thanks for letting me make amends."

He looked over his shoulder and then back at Mary. "The guys are here," he said. "They're calling me, so I guess I can go now."

Nodding, Mary smiled at him. "Bill's a great guy," she said softly. "And his family should be proud of him."

"Thanks, Mary," he said. "Thanks a lot."

Chapter Fifty

Light filtered down through the leaves on the trees, dappling the grass and leaf covered earth with golden light. Mary, Bradley and Chris slowly walked through the woods trying to find signs of makeshift graves. Birds sang in the trees, and a soft wind whistled through the tree limbs. The sky was bright blue with a few puffy, scattered clouds lingering lazily on the horizon.

"This doesn't feel like a graveyard," Bradley said.

They followed a set of large tire tracks that scarred the pristine ground and disappeared over a hill about forty yards ahead.

"I think they probably buried them over that hill," Chris said. "Close enough to be handy but far enough away from the house that no one would notice the constant excavation."

"I wonder how many people are buried here," Mary said. "They've been doing this for a number of years."

They reached the rise a few minutes later, and Mary gasped, leaning against a tree. Bradley came to her side and held her hand, wanting to see what she had seen. The small valley looked like a construction site. Upturned raw earth was everywhere. The trees had been plowed down to make room for pile after pile of small, rectangular hills with small tufts of grass and weeds growing between them. However, Mary was blind to the landscape. All she saw were the children. There were at least thirty little girls walking together, hand in hand, slowly climbing up from the desolate burial ground towards Mary. Facing the sunrise, the girls were bathed in sunlight, their features indiscernible.

Seeing a thick tree log about ten feet in front of them, Mary moved forward and sat there, hoping to present a less threatening posture to the children. "Hello," she said softly. "My name is Mary, and I want to help you go home."

From the middle of the group, one of the girls separated herself and came forward even as the others seemed to be wary and kept their distance.

A cloud drifted over the morning sun, and Mary was able to see the little girl's face more clearly. "Liza," she called. "I'm so happy to see you."

Liza walked the few more feet to Mary's side and stared at her for a moment. "Something's different," she said simply.

Mary nodded. "Yes, we were able to catch the bad man and his wife," she explained. "They won't be able to hurt little girls anymore."

"Did God send them?" she asked.

"No," Mary said vehemently, tears burning her throat. "God did not send them. God doesn't work like that. He works with love and compassion and patience. The bad people lied to you. They had nothing to do with God."

Liza leaned forward towards Mary's ear and whispered. "No one loves us. No one wants us."

Her heart breaking because she couldn't hold Liza in her arms and comfort her, Mary shook her head and met the little girl's eyes. "I promise you that God wants you and loves you," she said. "He wants you to come home so He can hold you in His arms and take away all of your pain."

"Are you sure?" she asked.

"I am," Mary said confidently. "Yes, I am."

Liza looked uncertain. She turned back to the girls on the hill and then looked at Mary. "What do we need to do?" she asked.

Mary took a deep, unsteady breath and wiped the tears from her cheeks. "Well, what I'd like you to do is have everyone come up here and talk to me for just a few minutes so I can get everyone's name and any information about who their families used to be," she said. "And then we'll be ready to let you go home."

"Will it be nice? Home?"

"Nicer than anything you ever experienced here on earth," she promised, knowing that statement probably held little comfort to the child who had never had much happiness during her short, five year stay. "And you will never have to be sad or frightened again."

Liza just stared at her again and sighed in a sad, resigned manner as if she really didn't believe things would get better but no longer had the strength to fight. "Okay, I'll tell the others."

Soon the rest of the girls joined Liza at the top of the hill and told Mary their information. Several of the girls didn't speak English, but between Mary, Bradley, and Chris's various bits and pieces of foreign language experience they were able to get the basic information gathered.

When the last child had answered her questions, they all stood around the log and looked at Mary. "What do we do now?" Liza asked.

Surprised they hadn't started to pass over, Mary was starting to worry when Mike appeared next to her. "Sorry I'm late," he whispered.

"Late? I don't understand," she said.

"You will," he said sending her a quick wink as he moved into the midst of the children. "Hi, I'm

Mike, and I'm an angel. I work for God, and he sent me here to help you get home."

The girls didn't seem convinced, and some even nervously stepped away from him.

"The thing is," he continued, not upset by their actions. "God realizes that bad things happened to you and that you're frightened. And he doesn't want you to be frightened anymore, so he is sending an escort for each one of you to guide you back home. Look."

Mike pointed up to the sky, and suddenly there seemed to be a flock of white doves circling the woods. They circled several times and then, one by one, drifted down to earth. But before they touched down, they changed from a dove to a beautiful angel dressed in white robes with large, white wings. The angels not only spoke in the languages of the girls but they also looked like they were the same nationality as the child. They greeted the children with smiles and words of comfort. Eyes wide with awe, the children eagerly went to the angels and then, enfolded in giant wings, they were securely taken home.

"That was beautiful," Mary said, her voice thick with emotion. "It was perfect."

"I'm not done yet," Mike replied.

And he was right. Mary realized there was one child left. Liza.

"I asked God if I could bring you home," he said, squatting down next to her. "You were the hero. You helped us discover all of the other girls who were lost, too. But if you're uncomfortable, I can send for another angel to come and get you."

She studied him for a moment and then stepped forward, wrapping her arms around his neck. Mike held her in his arms and stood, turning to Mary.

"I'll be back," he said, tears running down his cheeks, "as soon as I see Liza safely home."

Chapter Fifty-one

Mary stood outside the hospital room, very unsure of her welcome. "I don't want to be here," she whispered to Bradley, who was standing next to her. "I hate hospitals."

"She asked to see you," he whispered back. "That's got to be a good sign."

"Is she still armed?" Mary asked.

Before Bradley could answer, the door opened, and a nurse walked out. "Are you Mary?" she asked.

"Yes," Mary replied.

"Thank you for coming," the nurse said. "She's been pretty frantic about seeing you. You can go in now."

Mary grabbed Bradley's hand in a death-defying grip. "I need him to come in with me," she said, "for moral support."

The nurse nodded and held open the door for both of them.

Mary entered with the same reverence she would have felt if she had been walking into a chapel. She understood, more than most, that hospital rooms were often portals between this life and the next. Chief Chase, no, Mary corrected herself, Chelsea lay on a white sheet and pillowcase with a myriad of tubes and lines attached to her body. The monitor on the left side of the bed blinked reassuringly as her heart beat was registered in electronic cadence. An IV stand was on the right side of her bed with several plastic bags hanging from it, all filled with various hues of liquids flowing from the stand into her body.

She approached the bed, not knowing what to expect. "Chelsea," she whispered quietly. "It's Mary."

Eyelids fluttered open, and Chelsea took a moment to focus on Mary's face. "Mary," she croaked. "Thank you for coming."

"Sure, no problem," Mary replied. "What do you need?"

"I'm sorry," Chelsea breathed. "So sorry. I saw…I saw…"

Mary nodded. "I know you saw Mike," she said. "He told me."

"I saw…my…my mom," she said. "She died…when I was small."

"Oh, I'm so sorry," Mary replied, thinking about her own mother and how she would feel if she didn't have her in her life. "That must have been hard."

"I was angry," she continued. "If…if ghosts were real…why hadn't…why hadn't she come to me?"

"It doesn't always work that way," Mary replied. "I'm sure she would have come if she could."

Chelsea nodded slowly and smiled. "She told me…told me I needed to stay. Told me she would be watching over me. Told me she had always been there."

Mary nodded. "Yeah, that's what moms do," she agreed.

Chelsea moved her hand, trying to reach Mary. Mary took Chelsea's hand in her own. "Please forgive me," Chelsea said.

Mary smiled down at her. "Of course," she replied. "Now rest and get better because I want all the dirt on Mike so I can tease him."

Chelsea smiled and nodded. "You've got it," she whispered. "Thank you."

Mary slipped her arm into Bradley's as they walked down the hall together. "Well, I'm glad this day is nearly over," she said.

He glanced down at her. "Will you promise me never to chase a cold-blooded killer into an unstable tunnel again?" he asked.

"Yes, that's an experience I don't want to repeat," she agreed. "I'm going to find clumps of dirt in my hair for a month."

"Mary, I'm not ready to joke about this yet," he said. "When I saw the tunnel collapse around you, I thought my life had ended."

She paused and looked up at him. "I would have felt the same way," she said earnestly. "I'm sorry I frightened you. I was only thinking about not letting her get away."

"Um, excuse me for interrupting."

They both turned to see Chris standing in the hall next to them.

"Hi," Bradley said. "We were just in to see Chief Chase. She's going to recover."

"That's great news," he said. "I just wanted to let you know that the gunman, Gigi Amoretti, was found beneath several feet of dirt in the tunnel. They tried to revive her, but it was too late. They ended up pronouncing her dead at the scene."

"Thanks for letting us know," Mary said.

"Yeah, no problem," Chris replied. "Thanks again for your help."

They watched him walk down the hall in silence. Finally Bradley spoke, "I don't know what to say about that," he said. "I think it's a fitting end to a truly evil person, but it doesn't seem right to celebrate anyone's traumatic death."

Mary nodded. "Let's just not think about her anymore today," she said. "I just want to go home."

He hugged her. "Yeah, home sounds nice."

Chapter Fifty-two

The next morning Mary sat down at her desk and flipped the daily calendar page over to the next day. She chuckled softly as she looked down at the date of Friday the thirteenth. "So far so good," she murmured, and then she reached down and knocked on the wood surface of her desktop. "Knock on wood."

She accessed Liza's file, looked up Donna's phone number and placed the call. "Hi Donna," she said. "This is Mary. Mary O'Reilly. I wanted to let you know about Liza."

"Oh, hello Mary," Donna replied. "We already know about Liza. And we want to thank you for all you did."

"You know about Liza?" Mary asked, astonished. "How did you find out?"

"Oh, she came to visit Ryan last night," she replied. "He said she was beautiful again, and she was very happy. She thanked him for helping her and told him that she was happy."

"That's wonderful," Mary said, pulling a tissue from a box on her desk and blotting her eyes. "And how is Ryan doing?"

"He's doing great," Donna said. "He told me that he was going to miss her, but he was happy she finally got to go home."

"You've got a great little boy," Mary said. "And he's got a great mom."

"Thank you, Mary," Donna said. "And thank you for helping us. I really have learned a lot from this experience."

"Like what?" Mary asked.

"The most important thing I learned is that I've been afraid of things that really aren't all that frightening," she replied thoughtfully. "I think I need to look back on my life, on the decisions I've made based on fear and rethink them. I'm not going back to an abusive relationship. I know better than that. But I need to rethink things like going back to school or career choices. I think I need to be braver."

"Good for you," Mary said. "It not easy to be brave, but I think both you and Ryan will benefit from your choices."

"Yes, I think so, too," Donna answered. "Thanks again, Mary."

"You're welcome," Mary said. "Best of luck to both of you."

"Both of who?" Mike asked after Mary hung up the phone.

"Donna and Ryan," Mary replied. "Liza visited Ryan last night to say goodbye and let him know she was okay."

"Nice," Mike said. "I'm glad she got to do that."

"By the way, I had a nice conversation with Chelsea yesterday afternoon," Mary said. "I think she's finally getting over you."

Mike sighed. "It's hard to carry the guilt of so many broken hearts," he replied. "But I just have to remind myself that it's not my fault I was so good-looking and charming."

"It's a tough job, but somebody has to do it," Mary replied sarcastically.

"Yes. Yes it is," he agreed.

Smiling, Mary leaned back in her chair and propped her feet up on the top of her desk. "So,

Prince Charming, why are you here and not hanging around the house?"

"Your house has been invaded," he said.

"Invaded?" she asked.

"Yes. With women," he replied. "Young ones, old ones, middle-aged ones. There are women all over the place."

"Oh, the party," she said.

"Yes, between your mom and Rosie, the kitchen smells like heaven but looks, literally, like hell. And Katie is doing some craft thing with Maggie and Clarissa, so there are glue guns and glitter everywhere," he said, shaking his head in mock irritation. "But that's not the worst part."

Mary grinned. "Oh, what's the worst part?"

"Their language," he said. "There's a hidden language that only women understand. They laugh at things I don't get. They raise their eyebrows knowingly. They communicate with only a nod of their heads. I tell you, Mary, it's a little creepy."

"Well, you can hang here for a little while," Mary said. "But you have to stay quiet so I can finish my paperwork."

Mike lifted his hand to his heart. "Scout's honor," Mike said. "I'll just sit over there in the corner and think quiet thoughts. Quiet thoughts."

"Excellent," Mary said, looking down at the paperwork. "Quiet thoughts."

Mike glided over to the corner and looked around for a moment. He was already bored. He turned to Mary who was chewing on her pencil eraser and studying a receipt. He sighed loudly, and Mary looked up. "Quiet thoughts," he called across the room.

She smiled quickly, nodded and then looked back down at the paperwork.

216

A moment later, the electric pencil sharpener growled to life. Startled, Mary jumped and looked across the room. Mike was sharpening a box of pencils he had pulled from her supply shelf. She cleared her throat loudly, and Mike looked her way.

"Oh, yeah, right," he said. "Quiet thoughts."

Mary put down her pencil and started to laugh. "Okay, Mike, you win," she said. "What would you like to do?"

"Can we take a drive to Krape Park?" he asked. "I would really like to see some kids. Some happy, normal kids playing with their parents."

Mary nodded, tears filling her eyes. "That sounds like a great way to spend a Friday afternoon," she said, turning off her computer and picking up her purse. "Let's go."

Chapter Fifty-three

Mary looked around the room, and her heart was filled with joy. In one corner Ian and Stanley were arguing about politics. In another, her father was giving Bradley advice in his usual, boisterous, Irish way. And in the kitchen, Rosie was busy shooing Mary's brothers away from the cupcakes until it was time to make the announcement. The Brennan children and Clarissa were listening to Gillian tell a story about real-life faeries, and Katie and Cliff Brennan were sharing a loveseat and cuddling like newlyweds. She leaned against her mother, whose arm was around her waist.

"Do you ever just stop, look around, and realize how blessed you are?" she asked.

Her mother smiled softly, amused that her daughter's thoughts so closely mirrored her own. "Every day, darling," she replied. "Every day."

Mary turned and kissed her mother's cheek. "Thank you for being such a great mom," she said. "I've come to realize it's harder than it looks."

"Well, darling, I'd like to say that you made it easy," Margaret replied. "But that would be a bold-faced lie."

Mary laughed. "That's okay, Ma," she said. "You don't have to spare my feelings."

She saw Mike standing on the staircase watching the whole group from a distance and smiled at him. He smiled back, but it was a more somber smile than she was used to.

"Excuse me, Ma," she said. "I need to run upstairs for a moment."

She quietly left the group and walked up the stairs, passing Mike. "Follow me," she whispered and continued on without missing a beat.

She walked to the end of the hall and leaned against the wall, waiting only a moment for Mike to appear next to her.

"Great party," he said.

"Yes, it is," she agreed. "Everyone I love is here. But one of them is not happy. What's wrong, Mike?"

He shook his head. "There are just some rumblings upstairs," he said.

Mary was confused. "Thunderstorms?"

Mike grinned. "No, further up," he replied.

"Oh, I get it," she nodded and raised her eyes to the ceiling. "Rumblings."

Nodding, his smile widened. "Yeah, just like that," he said.

"Well, you know what they say," she said.

He shook his head, totally charmed by her. "No, what do they say?"

"You shouldn't bring your work home with you," she replied sagely.

"This from the woman who has ghosts showing up in her bedroom?" he asked.

"They don't show up in my bedroom anymore," she replied. "You put an end to that." She paused, and her eyes widened. "Oh no, did that cause the rumblings? Did I get you in trouble?"

"This from the woman who just risked her life to return thirty little girls to heaven?" he questioned tenderly. "No, you most certainly did not get me in trouble."

"Even though I thought nasty things about Chelsea?"

He chuckled. "Even though."

"Can you be happy, Mike?" she asked. "I really want you to be happy tonight. I want everyone to be happy tonight."

He nodded. "Yes, I can be happy. I am happy," he corrected. "You are my family, Mary, and I am thrilled to be here for your announcement."

"Good," she said. "Now let's go downstairs and have some cupcakes."

She walked down the steps, paused halfway and leaned over the banister. "Who wants to see what's in the middle of those cupcakes?" she asked.

Rosie carried a cake plate with three cupcakes to the center of the room. "Here they are," she said.

Bradley met Mary at the steps and walked her over to Rosie. He picked up a cupcake and held it up like a wine goblet. "Here's to my lovely wife, Mary. Thank you for loving me. Thank you for agreeing to share my love forever. And thank you for increasing our love and our family."

Mary kissed him on the cheek and picked up her cupcake. "Here's to my handsome husband, Bradley. Thank you for loving me even though I scare the heck out of you from time to time. Thank you for agreeing to share my love forever. Thank you for allowing me to be the mother of Clarissa, whom I love with all my heart. And thank you for increasing our love and our family."

Then she picked up the third cupcake. "Clarissa, you need to be part of this, too."

Clarissa scurried to the center of the room and smiled up at her parents. Bradley winked down at her. "Okay," he said. "On the count of three. One. Two. Three!"

They all bit into their cupcakes so the center fillings were revealed and turned them to the rest of the people in the family.

"Blue!" Clarissa screamed. "We're going to have a baby boy!!!"

Bradley leaned over and gave Mary a blue frosting kiss on her cheek. "Happy baby boy," he said.

"Have you thought of a name?" Stanley asked. "I hear that Stanley is coming back in style."

When the laughter settled down, Mary nodded. "Yes, we have thought of a name," she said. "We'd like our baby boy to be called Michael Timothy Alden."

A look of delighted surprise appeared on Mike's face. "Me?" he asked Mary.

She nodded. "He'll be named after two men whom we love and admire. Mike Richards and Timothy O'Reilly."

Mary's father walked over to her and kissed her. "Well, thank you, darling," he said. "I can't tell you how pleased I am. Little M. Timmy O'Reilly. What a grand name."

"Alden," Bradley reminded him. "His last name is Alden."

"Oh, for sure it is," Timothy said with a wink. "But he'll be an O'Reilly through and through."

He walked over to the counter, picked up a cupcake and turned to Ian. "So, did you hear?" he asked. "Little Timmy O'Reilly Alden. A fine name. A fine name indeed."

While the rest of the guests picked up cupcakes, Mike glided over to them. "Are you sure?" he asked.

"Mike, this was one decision that we both came to immediately," Bradley said. "Of course we're sure. We couldn't ask for anything better than for our son to grow up just like you."

"Well, maybe let's not tell him about cheeks and tattoos, okay?" Mary teased.

Mike nodded. "Not until he's at least fourteen," he agreed with a smile.

"Cheeks and tattoos?" Bradley asked.

"You probably don't want to know," Mary said.

Mike shook his head. "Yeah, at least not until the baby's name is printed on the birth certificate."

He shook his head. "I still can't believe you're doing this," he said. "And I want you to know that I'm honored. Honored and humbled. I'll try to be the best namesake a boy could have."

"You already are," Mary said.

Chapter Fifty-four

The room was dark, and Mary was trying to understand why she was there. She had been there before, of that she was sure. But why was she there again?

She moved forward tentatively, trying to find an exit door or a light. She didn't feel afraid, but she knew she didn't really belong there. A low sound, like the thrum of a bass note, was pulsing in the background over some hidden speaker system. Everywhere she went, the sound was present. She continued forward and heard another sound, soft and whispered, in the distance, the sound of a child's cry.

Dismissing caution, she hurried forward toward the source of the sound. Running down dark corridors that turned and twisted, she became even more frustrated. Finding herself at a dead end, she turned back and found a staircase that hadn't been there before. She jogged up stairs and down stairs, still following the elusive cry. Finally, she arrived at a door at the far end of a narrow hall. Light flooded out from beneath the door and around the sides into the dark hallway.

She grasped the doorknob, but the door itself seemed to be shrinking. The opportunity to save the baby was becoming smaller and smaller. Suddenly she was in the room, but the cry was from the other side of the door. Someone was taking the baby away. She sat on the floor, her legs straddling the door on either side as she pulled on the doorknob with all her might.

The crying became more frantic. The baby was in distress. Mary yanked on the door. It finally broke open, but the doorway was too small for her to slip through. Lying on the ground, she peered through the opening and watched a shadowy creature carry the sobbing baby into the night.

"No!" she screamed, pushing her hand out through the opening. "No, bring me back my baby!"

Sitting up with a start, Mary inhaled frantically, trying to catch her breath. Bradley's arms were already around her, pulling her to him. "It's all right, Mary," he said, his voice thick with concern. "It was only a dream. It was only a dream."

She pulled out of his arms, met his eyes and shook her head. "No, Bradley. I think someone is trying to take our baby."

Author's note: While I was plotting the adventures for Mary in Book 13, a friend of mine sent me a Reuter's article from March 2014 about re-homing. It called to my attention the underground market where parents use online bulletin boards to offer adoptees to strangers. I had no idea these practices existed in the United States, and as I have spoken with friends and family, I find that many of them have never heard of this practice either. However, when I was researching this book, I actually found sites that still offered children to strangers, much like you would offer a puppy or a kitten.

As of early 2014, there were no Federal laws against re-homing, and according to the article, only four states (Colorado, Florida, Illinois and Wisconsin) were moving forward with legislation. This is not fiction. This is a practice that needs to be halted. Please talk to your government officials to alert them to this practice. Spread the word that there needs to be other, safer options for adopted children and their new families when there are adjustment issues. We can make a difference in a child's life.

Thank you,

Terri

About the author: Terri Reid lives near Freeport, the home of the Mary O'Reilly Mystery Series, and loves a good ghost story. She lives in a hundred year-old farmhouse complete with its own ghost. She loves hearing from her readers at author@terrireid.com

Other Books by Terri Reid:

Mary O'Reilly Paranormal Mystery Series:

Mary O'Reilly Short Stories

PRCD Case Files:

Eochaidh:

226

.

CPSIA information can be obtained
at www.ICGtesting.com
Printed in the USA
LVHW09s0740261018
594909LV00015B/499/P